RS

Darlings Mark and
Aspasia
(Can't spell usually
hope there aren't
too many in the book!

Love

A Jacana book

Katy.

GW00508204

The Track

Katy Bauer

JACANA

First published in 2003 by Jacana Media
5 St Peter Rd
Houghton
2041
South Africa

ISBN 1-919931-13-9

Cover design by Disturbance
disturb@mweb.co.za

Printed by Fishwicks, Durban

See a complete list of Jacana titles at www.jacana.co.za

Table of Contents

Prologue

*T*here is a land near the southern tip of Africa that either floods or thirsts. Like a houseplant God forgets about then over-waters to make good. The people who lived there a hundred years ago fared the same way – wealthy one day, destitute the next. When the rich got poor the poor starved and it seemed God forgot his creatures too. But there was no time for mercy or compassion in that wet, arid Little Karoo.

Early pioneers walked there from the western mountains in search of grazing for their cattle. Others, of tougher complexion, accompanied them so as to soften the blow that it was to be alone in Africa. The rest came in dribs and drabs, merchants, blacksmiths and labourers looking to serve.

When the first white settlers reached a flat plain at the foot of a great black mountain range, they stayed, and when one of their number – a minor aristocrat named Baron Pieter van Rheede van Oudtshoorn – died there, they named the spot in his honour.

Among the reasonably cosmopolitan array of settlers were Jews running from Latvia and Lithuania to a better life in America. But when the ships to the New World were full, unscrupulous souls dealing in tickets for long distance voyage, crammed their persecuted countrymen onto ships destined any which way – some for Africa's most southern tip.

Amid the chaos and anxiety of boarding, the travellers were easily conned and often learned their new home's name once there was no longer any of the old in sight.

In Oudtshoorn, the Jews who could afford it were allowed to buy some of the undesirable strip of land at the very foot of the Black Mountains – Die Swartberge. The shadowy slopes were suitable for neither crop planting nor anchoring cattle, and so the new landowners captured and domesticated the huge prehistoric earthbound birds that roamed the area, and harvested their plumes instead.

Soon many Afrikaans and some English cattlemen kept ostrich too. The very large birds had very small brains and were relatively simple to farm. Less than two years after hatching they were fully grown; they weren't fussy eaters, they rarely became ill, and on their backs they flaunted what all the women of Europe and America desired be strapped to their heads.

Within two decades the fashionable feathers had made hundreds of mostly illiterate peasants rich. This thriving industry demanded imports and exports that moved swifter than a donkey trap. And so it was that the railway came to Oudtshoorn.

The Track

The track nestled in the stiff yellow grass, invisible from most angles, though somehow everyone knew exactly where it was. It was a magnet. People built homes near the track, they congregated at the track, they walked the track, they made love on the track, and on Saturdays – and some other days too – they would lie in the sun, drink too much, and fall asleep on the track. For most, those two silvery threads were the only evidence of that far-off industrial age they longed to touch, but were mostly too poor to reach.

The greatest harbingers of the locomotives were young boys with old faces who would fall down in the veld and press their ears to the line whenever one was about due. The greatest boast was to be the first to sense the train's approach and the last to leap away as it passed. The boys felt involved with the railway because of it, but rail travel was not for everyone. Most couldn't afford the fare and, besides, had nowhere to go, so they would stand close to the rails and glimpse the unimaginable glamour of the leather and mahogany interior of the passenger cars as they passed. At night the intoxicating effect was further enhanced by the glow of gaslight that shimmered off glass, jewels and teeth within.

It was the rich ostrich farmers and their families who had somewhere to go, usually Port Elizabeth or Cape Town, where great ocean liners waited to sail them away from that desolate landscape for as much as a year at a time. The rest just looked on, longingly, so tired of their wretched lives that occasionally one would propel themselves into the path of that exclusive escape mechanism rather than continue in the place where they were.

Death

The first feather boom died only eleven years after it hit. Greedy farmers and even greedier export merchants had allowed the market to become over-saturated. The crash left most of the ostrich men bankrupt, and with the money gone, life in the region dulled considerably.

The van der Want family was one of the few who survived the crash. A simple brood, and illiterate, they were sullen, kept to themselves, and regarded trips into town as almost decadent. They supplied a small number of plumes to the market and made a living that could have brought them a fair degree of comfort had they wanted it. They did not, and by the time the first boom was over, the finery and pretensions that had sunk other farmers had eluded them entirely.

The family of four lived in a two-roomed cottage eight miles west of Oudtshoorn. It was built on a flat, windswept piece of waste which lacked any shield against the elements. There were no trees and no mountains. Because the location was so barren, van der Want had bought the land cheaply and twenty-two years later, he had done not one thing to soften his landscape. Not one tree did he plant, no garden of any sort, no colour, no fresh paint. The home was little more than a shelter, a cramped, stinking barn for human animals. Their clothing and possessions could have been mistaken for those of paupers. Christmases and birthdays were marked by an absence of gifts. But frugal living eventually paid off, and when the first crash came, unlike those waltzing on credit, a considerable amount of cash bulged at the centre of Mammie and Pappie van der Want's loveless mattress as well as in Oudtshoorn's Standard Bank.

But Magda and Jacobus van der Want were only able to enjoy a miserly victory couple of months before both contracted a bizarre strain of influenza (the body puffed, the face grew blue spots), lay atop that stack of loot, and sneezed and shivered themselves to death, one within a week of the other.

The couple's bodies were barely cool when their sons Pieter and Hendrik started fighting over their inheritance. The van der Want farm was not very big and not very fancy, but it was all the brothers had and as they refused to farm together – having nurtured a loathing of one another all their lives – the land had to be divided. But there was only one source of water on the dusty patch.

When Pieter reported his brother missing to the local police just fifteen days after his parents' funeral, everyone relished suspicions of foul play, feeding off the slops of darkness they had always believed oozed from the devilish survivor.

But the matter was only briefly investigated and then dropped. In truth, no one could bear to question Pieter van der Want. He was so tall it was difficult to see his eyes, and those who did fix upon them soon looked away. The dull blue orbs were set deep into the skull and sat too close to the enormous nose which hung down past wide, floppy lips. The mouth was embedded in a bush of black hair, never combed and never cut, and the like on his head, chopped with a knife by van der Want himself perhaps once a year, appeared to hover around his great head rather than grow from it.

Even as a child he was an unsettling figure. A giant for his age, devoid of childlike qualities. The townspeople who glimpsed him on their travels into the country created folklore around him: his mother had squeezed a grumpy Colossus from between her legs rather than a baby. He had a tail. He could pick his father up and hold him above his head aged three.

Rural education at the time was generally conducted at home if at all, and required no books other than the family Bible. (That ominous volume more often wielded as a threat than a comfort.) Farm children were isolated as a consequence and in Pieter van der Want's case, the anti-social behaviour of his parents further layered his loneliness. Only once did he attempt to engage other children: Pa van der Want had taken the little Colossus to market on the outskirts of Oudtshoorn. Pieter was five years old though he looked nine. He wandered away from his father and loitered, intrigued, at the edge of a game of hopscotch. But Pa knocked him about the head before he could participate and the children laughed and called names after the dragged-away boy.

By the time Pieter was seven years old, any heart he was born with had frozen over and an active loathing of his fellow man consumed him. His family noted his aberrance about as much as they did their own. His older brother Hendrik was no playmate either and before Pieter grew tallest, the elder loved to twist and pummel and half drown his sibling.

Torture

$\mathcal{O}$nly the youngest Van der Want ever knew what happened to his brother; it was something he remembered almost fondly whenever he saw a fire burning in a tin drum.

When they were children, many of the torture rituals Hendrik van der Want exercised on his brother took place in a crater about two-hundred feet wide which lay beyond the dam at the farthest edge of the farm. The dip was perfect. It concealed cruel visuals, and it absorbed dire groans. The sessions were usually planned. Hendrik placed various instruments of pain at the spot beforehand so that all he had to do was drag his brother there and proceed.

The day Pappie and Mammie van der Want died, the younger sibling revisited the place. It had been six years since his brother had been strong enough to brutalise him, but Pieter had avoided the area nonetheless. Now, at dusk, when he knew he was about to take his revenge he returned.

The sunset made the red earth glow orange, and in the breeze the grasses swayed like flames. Pieter van der Want stood at the rim of the dolorous ditch. Most of the area was in shadow, but in the slice that was not yet dark, a rope and a loop of rusted barbed wire appeared as a grim reminder of the wounds they had once inflicted.

Van der Want looked at the inanimate objects a moment then let out a laugh. It was not a sound that he emitted very often and it shocked him a little, so he stopped. But he kept grinning and moved over to the objects, picked them up, and then laughed again anyway. Without human malice to wield them they were fairly harmless.

Anyway, they were in his power now.

Once his eyes became accustomed to the shade Van der Want noticed other things his brother had once used to break him: a splintered plank, a length of chain, a drum for making fire, shards of shattered glass.

That night Pieter and Hendrik dragged their dead parents out into the shed and slept soundly on the precious mattress themselves. They would bury their dead in the morning – it was winter, the bodies would keep. Early the following day the brothers interred their kin without ceremony, without even bothering to identify which body lay where, then started to argue about their inheritance. Within minutes tongues had turned to fists, but now it was Pieter who had premeditated the violence.

With the rusted piece of barbed wire around his neck and his brother tugging hard at the ends, Hendrik van der Want tottered towards the donga. Pieter said nothing, Hendrik only gurgled. Neither had ever known words to be of any use for anything. Once down in the hollow the captive was slashed, burned, and beaten to its end. It was then tipped head first into an oil drum and set alight, bloodied boots poking almost comically from the rim.

Pieter diligently fuelled the fire for an hour, then when burning fat took over he settled down to doze and dreamed of nothing at all while the whiff of his scorching brother wafted up to his nostrils.

With one body still smouldering and two fresh in the ground, Van der Want rode into town to report the death of his parents and the disappearance of his brother. He told the police and he told the bank. Influenza had killed so many people that the police couldn't fuss about a couple of peculiar farming folks buried without any official death certificate. As for the brother, they took down Pieter's grunting replies to their questioning and said they would keep an eye out for him, then said "Good day". They wanted the man they hated to look at out of the station as quickly as possible.

Van der Want then went to the bank. A terrified eighteen-year-old teller, whose belly said he ate too much and whose skin flaked like pastry, said: "Just a minute sir," then dashed to the manager's office where, too flustered to speak, he simply shuddered and pointed back out towards the counter. Bank manager Patrick Bloomfield, a jumpy man at the best of times, twitched out to the banking hall pushing the clerk before him. He recognised Van der Want at once and flushed a tense orangey brown. "Please, yes, Mr Van der Want, come through," he managed thinly. Van der Want strode into the back office, sat opposite the nervy manager, and tossed the police form – which he himself was unable to read – onto the desk in front of him. Bloomfield blinked up and down at the paper and tried to dodge Van der Want's malevolent gaze.

"I'm sorry for your news. Yes, this is from the police but do you have the death certificate Mr Van der Want? From a doctor? Do you have an identity document, for yourself? And your brother you say is missing?"

When Bloomfield's enquiries met with no more than a series of barely perceptible movements of the wild, matted, simian head before him indicating the negative, he continued hurriedly as if all had been in order anyway.

"Yes, well, normally we would need that, but I understand that in these terrible times with the 'flu being so bad, these things don't always work out as conveniently as we would like. No, they don't."

Bloomfield scrutinised the deposit book Van der Want had given him, as if he hoped it might contain some magic formula which would assist him through the encounter. It did not and Bloomfield's will to continue with the interview failed him.

"Yes, well I think that's fine then. We'll make all the necessary changes."

Van der Want left the bank. The manager wiped his face. The flaking clerk with the angry skin emerged from the bolted latrine ten minutes thereafter.

There was plenty of gossip, but the police found no evidence to support the town's conviction that a murder had been committed. Of course they never found the brother of Pieter van der Want, but what could they do?

Romance

*W*ith the inheritance now all his own Van der Want was able to sell the farm, swap twenty fully-grown ostrich for forty chicks and move away. Away from the town's people: the people who had told the police to question him, the people who had parties and never invited him, the people who went to church but never prayed for him. Where Van der Want was going, nobody would stare at him. There would be no parties, no questions, no God. He would buy so much land that he alone would watch and judge. But first he needed a wife.

Erma van Gass was the only daughter of a neighbouring farmer. Old Man van Gass had been Old Man van der Want's only friend, and it was on a rare visit from the former to the latter that Pieter first saw his future wife. One look was enough for him to know she was perfect: plain and mute, possibly because she was never addressed, possibly because she was shy but most likely because she was afraid. Her lank brown hair hung loose to her shoulders and framed a face like dough, distinguished only by a large, purple birthmark which stretched all along her left jawbone. No man would ever try to steal such a wife, and no such wife would ever have the spirit to leave her husband.

Van der Want was largely correct in his summation of the girl. Already nineteen, she had never been to a dance or heard an admiring word from anybody, man or woman. Like Van der Want, she had been isolated as a child and taunted by her brothers who found the raspberry coloured splash across her jaw an endless source of crude amusement.

Her only hope for female sympathy lay with her Ma, but that was a doomed desire. In fact the most powerful thing Erma possessed was her quiet insanity, which – due to her ability to function and obey in a robotic fashion unremarkable enough to be taken for 'normal' – nobody ever realised.

Almost a year after spotting Erma van Gass, and with all his family dead, Van der Want rose at four one morning, stacked a wagon with supplies, left by six and arrived at the three-roomed Van Gass farmhouse one hour thereafter.

Like everything else in the Little Karoo, the seasons were extreme. Summers scorched all living things, and winters froze them. Van der Want found the family that icy June morning – mother, father and three hulking sons – sitting idle but for their shivering, gleaning whatever heat they could from a small fire burning in an enormous hearth. The boys, all blonde, ruddy, and fat like Ma, were virtually indistinguishable from one another, their features equally crude. They were also cursed with a common sinusitis which they snorted and huffed and spat energetically. It was a repulsive din which they kept up on a rota basis. Occasionally, all three GRRRUU-PHTH-T!-ed at once, effecting a vile and startling crescendo. Pa van Gass squinted at the huge, dark figure in the doorway, which had appeared without knocking. "Van der Want," he growled.

"Ja," came the reply.

No one moved. All eyes remained on the fire. The indifferent response from a family visited no more than twice a year seemed normal to Van der Want, coming as he did from hardly more animated stock himself.

At first he didn't see Erma. Not that he particularly wanted to, other than to be assured that she had not been eaten by wild dogs, or, less likely, fetched to fix another man's dinner. Then something shifted at the other end of the room, and the visitor made out the emaciated figure of the girl, poised with a handful of sock to darn.

"I'm going now. I want to take Erma," said the visitor.

"You want to marry her?" said her father. Then without waiting for Van der Want's reply he added, "What for me?"

Although there appeared to be little difference between the Van Gass lifestyle and the Van der Want lifestyle, Van Gass had had no luck with ostrich birds and was poor and bitter because of it.

Van der Want handed over a small suede pouch. Ma van Gass screwed her large, terracotta face towards her husband's lap and watched him shake out silver amounting to two pounds (less than a quarter of the amount paid for an ostrich chick before the slump). Ma twisted again, this time to see her daughter. She nodded and the awkward waif rose and scuttled past Van der Want, who still had not moved from the doorway.

She gathered her clothes (a tiny bundle), her hat and her Bible from the adjacent room. Packing took no more than a hundred seconds. Then she glanced at her family who barely glanced back, and left with the man who had come to fetch her.

Marriage

The wedding was an unceremonious affair. A Dutch Reformed monolith on the road to Oudtshoorn provided an appropriate setting for a stern exchange of vows.

Churches were in no short supply in the region. As gathering places and bastions of the believed moral high ground, they were of interest to most people, however degenerate their own behaviour. The Van der Want clan were among the few who paid the institution no mind. The Van Gass family weren't much more interested, though a Bible being Erma's only possession (it came to her when a dishevelled drifter had died whilst crossing their farm) she treasured it. But now Pieter van der Want needed its ritual if he was to secure himself ownership of Erma van Gass.

The door of the church was unlocked. The interior was cold and empty. Van der Want began to snort with frustration at once, but then a figure in black suddenly shot its head and shoulders over one of the pews like a glove puppet, greasy grey hair plastered to its head like a coat of paint. It was Dominee De Jaager. He was drunk as usual, and had been lying down in one of the pews and thinking about how he would love to have that smart tweed suit he had seen in the window of Hatfields Department Store two days before.

His theological interest was scant. Poverty and a lack of options had forced him to take to the pulpit, and so he drank.

"Yes?" he asked.

"Can you marry us?" came Van der Want.

"Of course. Do you have any money?" asked de Jaager boldly, still unmoved from his popped-up position in the pew.

"Ja."

Now de Jaager squinted. His eyes were not good. His spectacles had broken during a sottish tumble two years before and had still not been replaced. He had pretended to read from the Bible ever since. He could read the chapter name in bold at the top of the page, and remembered enough of what it was about for the uniqueness of his version to have gone largely unnoticed by his mostly illiterate flock.

He squinted, pulled himself out into the aisle and jerked towards the couple. As he drew nearer he realised that what he had taken for one man sitting on another man's shoulders was in fact just one man, and that the child he thought stood beside him, was in fact a woman. Despite the lack of beauty in the local population, de Jaager realised that these two were particularly malformed, and he, who spent a fair deal of his time fantasising about beautiful things he would never afford, was repulsed. The unexpected interruption combined with the heat and the liquor make him suddenly nauseous and he rushed outside to gag. One of his parishioners whom he did not recognise happened to be passing at that very moment and moved off the road to see whether she might be of assistance to this retching man of God.

"Thank you ma'am," managed the Dominee feeling somewhat refreshed after the gag. "You can help. You can come in and bear witness to a small wedding ceremony for me."

In less than half an hour Mr and Mrs Van der Want were silently moving east once more.

Sex

$\mathcal{D}$esire had not enticed Van der Want to marry Erma van Gass. In fact, she repulsed him. But his sexual appetite was nonetheless tremendous.

He had fornicated with farm animals since he was a young boy, and had first experienced a woman at age eleven. Unlike most other farm boys, Van der Want's first intercourse with a human was not with a sibling, cousin or servant, it was with Isadora Bloomfield, wife of the nervy Standard Bank manager, Patrick.

Isadora Bloomfield had been a beauty when she had married her husband in England seventeen years earlier. The motivation for the match was not unusual for the time. The two had grown up next door to each other in a nice middle-class suburb of London. Although they'd never been great childhood friends, their families knew each other well enough and the marriage seemed likely to work due to common ritual if nothing else.

Isadora's infatuation at the time of her engagement with a married man was never revealed to her beau, and she was encouraged by her lover to accept the proposal as it provided a convenient excuse for him to end the affair. Devastated but sensible, Isadora agreed, besides she'd heard no end of glamourous tales about colonial wives being waited on day and night, passing their time either hunting big game or socialising. She loved adventure as much as she loathed household chores, and clear skies would make a change from London smog. So she accepted Patrick Bloomfield's proposal and looked forward to life in Africa. Her husband, who neither repelled or attracted her, was more or less a secondary consideration.

By her mid-thirties twelve years of heavy drinking had added twenty to her looks, and the fine Karoo dust seemed to have settled into that formerly radiant skin, lending her face a pallor of putty grey.

Her nationality, habits, and religion combined to make her lonely in Oudtshoorn. There was no glamour in this part of Africa that she could see. Kenya was where the lions were. The town's social life revolved around the church rather than the dance hall, but even in this she was afforded no succour. The dominant Dutch Reformed parish considered her method of seeking God's grace nothing short of heresy. "Die Roomse gevaar", the Roman danger, they hissed as she passed.

In an attempt to comfort herself, Isadora spent much of her time consuming ever larger quantities of food and drink and she swelled considerably as a result. But she always took pride in her appearance, and would start each day clean and perfumed, wearing some or other large, pretty dress.

She was a forlorn rather than a furious lush, her voice and features tending to soften with the liquor. Her balance when inebriated was remarkable, and her speech remained on the whole light and unslurred. It was her hair that gave her away. The drunker she'd become, the more she would prod at the great mass of yellow pinned up top. Her aim was to keep the hairdo neat, but instead the bun, which started off near the centre of her skull, shifted further to the left and down until the clump of dead matter rested just above her plump powdered cheek.

Because she refused to remain indoors all day, as her husband had urged more than once, Mrs Bloomfield's drinking was no secret in Oudtshoorn. She even frequented public bars unaccompanied. This was especially disgraceful, and she was especially scolded, but when she was shopping in town for the likes of wax or ham, she could hardly resist veering off to the Golden Plume, where the well-tipped barman could not resist pouring her gin.

It was a dismal affair, and yet the Bloomfields continued to receive invitations to many of the fanciest dinners in town, though they were extended less for the pleasure of the couple's company than the reassurance that the credit which had made the feast possible would continue to flow.

It was not unusual at such gatherings, for the manager's wife to enjoy the wine more than she should and then doze at table. In response her husband would utilise the only weapon he had left against his wife's dipsomania: denial was his ordinance and although it had no sharp edges, he wielded it as deftly as if it had. "My dear, you seem tired," he'd say to the back of his snoring partner's head, "Let me take you home."

Invariably a clattering of cutlery on crockery would ensue as the sober spouse and perhaps one chivalrous gent would help the lady to her feet, carry her past gloating guests, and out.

When Isadora Bloomfield had her fateful encounter with young Pieter van der Want it was January and too hot to live. Cactuses drooped and lizards gasped. Around lunchtime she was refused a drink at The Plume – the barman having been better tipped by her husband half an hour earlier. She glugged the last of her domestic supply that morning and being unable to get service in any of the town's other drinking establishments, she trudged, as calmly as she could, to the bank, took her husband's horse and buggy from where it was tied up outside, and drove herself out of town in search of refreshment elsewhere.

She'd heard about bars in the wilderness run and frequented by coloureds, and was determined to find one.

Two hours later, Isadora was lost. Her throat was as crisp as toast. She'd thought so hard about gin, she'd forgotten to take any water with her and the parched landscape was suddenly all mirage. Isadora felt that death had come to her and she was glad of it. She jerked the horse to a standstill, rolled off her perch, sought shade beneath the carriage, and waited for meek, merciful, Mary to appear. Mother of

Christ would surely scoop her up in her cobalt wrap and whisk her away from that bad life to a place so sublime it would feel like she was drunk all the time.

She was woken about an hour later by a six foot tall, eleven-year-old boy. Pieter van der Want had been to buy supplies for Pa from a trader who lived down river. About three miles from home he spotted the carriage.

Up close all he saw of the lady at first was one black leather boot and an inch of floral hem. He dismounted his horse and kicked the foot. When this failed to rouse the body he crawled under the wagon and threw a little of his water on the lifeless face. Isadora came to and snatched the bottle from his hands. She gulped hard twice, then stopped suddenly. "Haven't you got any gin?" she asked. The boy just stared. The English woman was quite used to this sort of response, and had mastered a few drinking terms in Afrikaans specifically for such an emergency. She asked the question again, this time making different sounds. Now the boy lumbered off to his horse and came back carrying the new bottle of brandy meant for Pa. The stranger sucked on the liquor much harder than she had on the water. Three, four, five, six, gulps, and when it looked like she would never stop, Pieter grabbed her hair in one hand, the bottle in the other and yanked them apart.

Isadora didn't move. She closed her eyes and poked once at her terribly dishevelled head. She smiled faintly and forgot about the boy. She forgot where she was. She just lay there, singing softly something which might have been *Ave Maria*, might have been *Hush-a-bye-Baby*, and enjoyed the feeling of drunkenness that began to glow in her belly once more. Pieter didn't move either. He liked the wanton look about this lady in disrepair. He'd only ever seen coloured women look like that, but you wouldn't touch them unless you wanted your hand chewed off. Should he treat her like any other animal, find a hole and have his way? Would it be any different? Any different from a chicken or a donkey? Van der Want's needs were gross as ever, but his hesitation was unique. He could overpower her, but perhaps he wouldn't have to. So he stayed and stared a minute. When his muse opened her eyes she noted the way the boy looked at her and didn't mind.

There had been no sex in the nuptial Bloomfield bed for several years. When his wife seemed unable to fall pregnant, the bank manager decided there was no point in continuing with the messy business of trying to make her so. Isadora's dejection grew, but her frustration led to nothing more than a couple of mildly embarrassing flirtations with men more fearful of scandal than immorality who kissed her then rebuffed further advances.

The lady undid the top ten buttons of her dress, revealing part of a pink satin corset which oozed plenty of soft white flesh. Her enormous breasts spilled so far over the rim that the tops of her nipples were exposed. Pieter's groin throbbed like never before as he plunged his face into that milky cleavage.

The two never met again. They never even knew each other's names. After sex, Mrs Bloomfield requested and received another five gulps of brandy and was escorted back to the edge of Oudtshoorn by the boy.

Isadora Bloofield died five months later during a miscarriage. Pieter van der Want was beaten because of the missing brandy.

The Journey

Van der Want skirted Oudtshoorn on his journey east with his new wife. He had avoided going into town most of his life and was not about to do so now just because his bride had the temerity to suggest that they might.

"I do," were the only two words that had passed Erma's lips since she'd left her family home. With Oudtshoorn in sight she thought hard before she said, "Don't we need supplies from Oudtshoorn?" He wanted to slap her for asking, but he controlled himself, afraid she might try to run off within view of the town. So he said nothing, just kept steering the horses away.

So they travelled without speaking. At night Erma made food while Van der Want watered the horses and fed the ostrich chicks. Then he'd take the woman by the arm, motion her into the wagon and violate her as many times as his balls would bear it.

Erma said nothing, but each night once her husband's breathing had slowed she moved outside the wagon, gathered stones and twigs and grasses and performed small, damning, satisfying rituals which she believed would help harm the monster eventually.

At dusk on the sixth day, Van der Want stopped the wagon and settled on the land he had bought a month before. He named the deserted valley Vlakteplaas.

Agatha

$\mathcal{L}$ady Agatha Teeling-Smith's intelligence, manner, capabilities, judgement, and taste were nothing short of formidable. She was the second of five girls. Her sisters all had soft, delicate faces, which contrasted dramatically with their hard, manipulative natures. Neither Agatha's face nor personality could have been described in the same way.

She was tall and her shoulders were too broad. Her features were handsome rather than pretty. There was just too much of her. In addition to these physical drawbacks, she could never manage flirtation and was far too intelligent to enjoy the preferred clichés expressed by the young men of her day. In short, the qualities Agatha did possess were considered highly unattractive in a young lady near the end of the nineteenth century. It all horrified her mother, and it all delighted her father.

The daughter was not entirely unconventional. She liked music and flowers and co-operated enthusiastically with many of the things her mother held dear to her heart. What sort of tea set was appropriate for what sort of weather, that type of thing, but she would not embrace some of Mama's weightier rules, mainly who to invite to drink tea from which tea set and it was enough to create an undesirable air of eccentricity about her.

At twenty-five, Agatha eloped with a man three years her junior. As far as the lovers were concerned, the match was made in heaven. But the families on both sides were less impressed. Her people were Scottish, upwardly mobile and astonishingly rich. His people were

English, titled and living way beyond their means on money filched from the Scots two centuries before. The consequent contempt between the clans left the lovebirds just one option for a peaceful future: a move to the colonies.

Lord Humphrey Teeling-Smith was devoted to the inspection of rocks. This geological sense of purpose made Africa a more appealing prospect than Asia, the south promised to be more venerable than the north, and Oudtshoorn had caves, the great Cango Caves. And so the choice of new home was decided.

"Humphrey is a trrrrroglodyte!" his wife would trumpet in an astonishing mixture of fine English and formidable Scots.

"When he's home, I hang umbrrrrellas from the ceiling, like stalactites in an attempt to entice him to stay beyond half an hour!"

Her humour was more often than not wasted on a non-comprehending audience in Oudtshoorn, but she didn't mind. She felt sure that one day, the glorious English tongue would be known to them all, and once they knew it, they could ponder whatever she said and do themselves a bit of good by it.

When they first arrived in that world of feathers, the Teeling-Smiths were anomalous. They were polar bears amongst camels, and it took some time before the local humped plodders stopped staring in wonder at the pale pair, swinging their heads from side to side in search of things as rare as ice.

But the bears were curious creatures, only vaguely thrown by the strangeness of the camels and the dust they hooved. The male scratched obsessively at pieces of stone, while the female busied herself weaving a sumptuous patch of northern hemisphere into the powdery African earth as if it were the most natural thing in the world to do. She also embarked on an endless cycle of importing furniture, books, fabric, and plants from Britain. The time this took was considerable but of no consequence to her in that parched geologist's dream. What did finally matter was the cost. The seemingly enormous lump sum of ten thousand pounds given to her and a smallish annual grant allowed him by their displeased kin would not support the couple's preferred lifestyle forever – not even in Oudtshoorn.

The reality of looming bankruptcy hit home when Agatha's husband died in a climbing accident aged thirty-seven. Nobody saw him fall, but the body was found within about forty-eight hours and his injuries clearly indicated the cause of death. Two days of Karoo summer had not been kind to Humphrey's remains, but Agatha bore the sight with considerable poise.

So the widow found herself alone, forty years old, with just five hundred pounds in the bank and six stone rooms crammed with finely-turned furniture. She was horrified by the loss of her most precious Humph. So many reminders about the place: pipe, spectacles, walking cane and those bits of rock she could never throw away. But the challenge of how to survive until her own departure was suddenly paramount.

A return to Scotland was out of the question. In the fifteen years she'd been away she'd received about as many missives from home. As her father had died shortly after her departure, they were all from her sister. All cold. All clearly motivated by a desire to punish Agatha for the choices she had made. Besides, fifteen years of strange adventure had made an unlikely African out of Agatha.

Before her husband's death Agatha had run an impeccable household; she banged tirelessly, and not too badly, at the pianoforte, and she had read and re-read hundreds of books. She made roses defy the dust, and tea a summer refreshment, but now she had to make money.

The prospect at first seemed a tedious one, but the more she mulled it over the more she came to like the idea of it. She discussed the matter with her friend, confidante and servant Nessie Plaatjies.

"Nessie! I need to make some money!"

"Oo no madam! Terrible business that. You don't need to do that madam. You richer than anyone anyway."

Nessie Plaatjies and Agatha had found each other in a park at the centre of Oudtshoorn one stifling Wednesday morning. Agatha's

Humph had been dead three weeks.

Nessie had a small bag of belongings with her. She had left her husband for the last time that morning and was quietly discussing the matter with – Agatha presumed – the birds. Another reason she took such an interest in the scene was that this toothpick of a woman occupied her preferred bench and she didn't look like shifting despite Agatha's confident approach. Indeed, having the most stately looking woman in Southern Africa halt by her side did not seem to disconcert the woman on the bench one bit, she just jerked her head upwards and said, "Hello."

Unused to this kind of reaction Agatha skipped a greeting and asked, "Are you going to be sitting there much longer?"

"Ja, probably hey."

"Really! What sort of an answer is that?"

"I don't know. But then I don't know about anything anymore. EXCEPT that men is a pain in the bum."

Agatha's shock made her laugh. What a curious little woman, brown as a berry yet sitting there in the park as if she owned it and addressing Agatha more like a neighbour than a servant.

Agatha could not bring herself to sit down next to the woman, but she did stay and listen to her story.

"I'm glad I left. I had to," said Nessie, summing up, "It wasn't because he was lazy and it wasn't because he was drunk, it was because he was so boring. He hardly ever said anything. It was making me crazy. I like to have a bit of a chat," she concluded, then followed up at once with, "Do you have a job for me maybe madam?"

Agatha immediately said "No," although she had felt short staffed for some time. Then suddenly remembering as much she said, "Yes".

"I know I look richer than anyone around here Nessie," said Agatha, "But the truth is simply that I am not. So I'm thinking of farming!"

"Oo now that's very funny. You going to get all your fine clothes messed up. I like that joke. You farming." Nessie giggled the rest of the day about it. But Agatha persisted and about five days into this sort of talk she had made up her mind. The plan was simple, she would do what hundreds of intellectually inferior men were doing all around her, she would farm ostrich.

"Madam, there's going to be a lot of angry men in this place if you do that. Oo that's funny madam! They not going to like it."

Nessie was right, the men didn't like it. At first they thought it quite amusing, this rich old English woman going to market, buying grain and all. But producing top quality plumes meant more than keeping a few giant birds alive. So when Agatha's pluckings yielded great puffs of white wonder fit to crown the Prince of Wales, well, there were enough sour grapes about to ruin a vineyard.

Agatha put her particularly speedy success down to nothing more than that she loved her birds. She would go down and sing to them every morning after breakfast, and she fed them treats although what these were remained her secret until the day she died.

More than one farmer tried to love their birds because of it, and when Agatha hinted that the creatures liked women, wives, daughters, nieces and others were coaxed down to the pens. Clothing was ripped, hats molested, gloves pecked at, and men very often slapped as a consequence.

Agatha made so much money that she weathered the first feather slump in relative style. Her extravagances were nothing compared to those of her competitors and her credit was good.

The first crash didn't last too long and eight years after the industry's demise it boomed bigger than ever before until an ounce of feathers was worth an ounce of gold.

Sara de Beer

$\mathscr{B}$ecause the wealth in Oudtshoorn belonged to several races (although no Khoi, San, coloured, or black) a variety of cultures thrived, and a veneer of tolerance was afforded to those who could afford it. However, as elsewhere in the Empire, it was the British who monopolised social standing, and it was this minority's customs that were considered most desirable to know among the wealthier farmers. British taste was exotic to the new millionaires, some of whom had been lapping tea out of bowls not long before, and everything from the language to the correct use of cutlery had to be mastered from scratch.

Of these skills Sara de Beer (a woman who was much molested by birds once her husband heard of Agatha's secret) was a particularly slow learner, but her resolve to triumph was unshakeable.

Sara was the only child of a couple who owned a small, general store in Port Elizabeth and were not well-off because of it. But Thys de Beer would change all that. A struggling twenty-nine year old cattle farmer at the time, de Beer was in town for the purpose of divorcing his first wife who had left him for a man wealthier than he some months before. The proceedings numbed rather than upset him and, as he left the courthouse, a sudden craving for tobacco consumed him.

On entering Sara's shop, de Beer noticed the bubbly eighteen year old behind the counter at once. He noted how different she was from his ex-wife: a cool, intelligent sort (too damn clever!) who hardly disguised her contempt for her husband's semi-literacy. In fact she joked about it regularly. It was his confidence, his fearlessness that had first seduced her, but she was bored within a year.

This one in the shop though, she was so opposite. More and more he relished her silliness as she flapped about the shelves. Her ridiculous comments, that came from nowhere and went back the same way, her nervous giggle, her flirtatious glances, all so clumsy, but the more she fluttered, the more it endeared her to him and by the time they'd completed their thrilling transaction, involving an ounce of tobacco, a pack of toothpicks and a ha'penny change, Thys de Beer had proposed.

Sara giggled and said that it would be nice, but that she'd have to ask her father first. The old man appeared from the back room where he'd been eating his lunch, wiping his mouth and beaming all at once. He thought it a grand idea. He was delighted at the prospect of being rid of the too chipper daughter who'd learnt all she knew from her mother whom he could sadly never imagine being fetched away so handily as this. "She's a wonderful girl. A wonderful girl. You have my blessing."

At twenty Sara was pretty, at forty plain, and by the time she was in her early fifties she was plain bulbous. So she flaunted the things for which she remained noteworthy: stupidity, a certain sweetness and excessive wealth. She was also sharp enough to realise that it was British custom that could best nurture these qualities and to this end Sara imported herself a teacher from England.

The teacher's name was Anne Sutton, and she was hired on the basis of a letter she had written in response to Sara's advertisement in a London daily stating her virtual obsession with the very best of British taste and custom.

Mrs de Beer had always wanted to be Lady Agatha Teeling-Smith – but in brighter clothes – and felt certain that Miss Sutton would make just such a transformation possible.

The hired help turned out to be so well versed in the ways of the British upper classes – despite her own lower middle-class origins –

she had even acquired the aristocratic knack of being thoroughly rude about anything which wasn't quite right. In short, she was a tyrant, and her eye wreaked havoc on the house of de Beer. Everything was wrong. The way the beds were made, the colour schemes, the food, even Mrs de Beer's dress sense left much to be desired. But far from being wounded, her mistress hung on her every word. As long as each insult was pre-empted with "in the best English houses" or "all the smartest ladies in London" the changes were made not so much willingly as happily, joyfully, hysterically! Sara giggled and blushed and seemed to delight in the put-downs.

One case in point was that of the scarlet shed: Sara had ordered a painstakingly beaded and embroidered gown to be made for her to wear to the society wedding of pretty young ostrich heiress Hettie Steyn and the outrageously handsome young buck Boetie Bruin. Their names were not all that rang lyrical, and the union of the glamourous young sweethearts captured the imaginations of everyone in Oudtshoorn who possessed one and many of those who did not.

The wedding was to be the most fashionable of the year, possibly the decade, and what to wear became the quintessential puzzle of the day. Sara spared no expense trying to ensure that the gown she wore would be uniquely exquisite, and as usual she flexed the notion that more was indeed more.

Anne Sutton's counsel was engaged throughout the process of course, and although she never said anything overtly complimentary Sara was glad to mistake her cool for smart British reserve. This, however, was a mistake, and the paragon of spite waited until the eleventh hour before fully expressing herself.

At the final fitting Sara could hardly be dressed her excitement shook her so. She was also slightly fatter than she had been a week earlier, which made it look as though her seamstress Mrs Broil was mugging rather than dressing her. Finally 'in', Sara, gasping for breath, turned from the mirror to face her harridan help. But Anne Sutton was silent. Sara decided that this was because the seamstress, who had been spitting an average of fifteen superlatives a minute through a mouthful of pins since their arrival, had spun the English servant into a ball of sulk. "Shhhhhh! Mrs Broil! Please," snapped Sara, then panting looked to Sutton once more for approval. But now the sulk was gazing through window. "Anne, what's the matter? Don't you liked my dress?" said Sara moving with some difficulty towards her. Anne kept her back to her mistress and sighed: "Well I suppose it will have to do," then turning sharply towards her victim, "I suppose I should have said something earlier, but you were so headstrong, as usual, and in fact never did consult me on the colour." Sara was beginning to hyperventilate. She clutched at her midriff and pleaded "What? What do you mean 'the colour'?" The dress was a strong red. Anne turned to the window once more shaking her head. "I don't know how else to tell you Madam so I'm just going to give you the benefit of my frankness as usual."

Sara was now beginning to swoon. "What?" she yelped. Mrs Broil let out a small "Eep!" and fell to whimpering. Anne turned towards the dress once more and perused it, the corners of her mouth stretched floorwards slightly more than usual. Her brow furrowed. Upset and perhaps a little disgusted, she lied: "Madam, it is exactly the same red that first Her Majesty the Queen and as a consequence many of the finest families in Britain have painted their garden sheds. It is in fact such a phenomenon, that shortly before I left England to come here, the society column of the London *Times* carried an article about it." Mrs Broil screamed, then bustled forward just in time to break the fall of her client.

Anne Sutton dropped to her knees and rolled Sara roughly off Mrs Broil, and onto her face, then set about loosening the offending garment. Mrs Broil pushed herself to her knees and shook with shock, squealing louder all the time. Anne Sutton left off unfastening a moment and slapped the seamstress' smooth chubby face quite hard then ordered a glass of water for Mrs de Beer.

Finally Sara's imprisoned midriff leapt to freedom like a large bullfrog from a schoolboy's pocket and she turned to face Anne – smiling and weeping all at once. "Anne, you is so clever. Thank you!" and she pulled the woman to her bosom. Quite bewildered and slightly nauseated, Sutton jerked herself and her employer up from the floor. Mrs Broil returned with the water but did not speak while Sara de Beer became profound. Holding Anne's hands like a lover, Sara looked into her helper's eyes and proceeded: "This is so wonderful, because we know this about the sheds and I also know that at least two other women in town, who wanted to copied me, ordered exactly this same fabrics for their outfits – AND NOW THEY WILL LOOK LIKE SHEDS!" she crescendoed. Things were still a moment. Anne Sutton retracted her feeble chin so far it disappeared entirely into her neck. A giggling Sara de Beer tramped vigorously out of the foul-coloured garment and started kicking it about the studio.

Such profligate behaviour did not bother Sara's husband, she was a good luck charm to him. Shortly after their wedding, a chance business transaction left him reasonably well off, and after that money came to Thys de Beer as easily as gastric wind. Soon he was plucking millions out of big bird's arses like nobody's business and in time became the wealthiest man in Oudtshoorn. He was also the town's mayor. A relentless self-publicist, photographs of himself surrounded by great fluffy plumes found their way into most of the town's public buildings, and several of its private ones too.

The son of a poor, Afrikaans farmer, Thys de Beer could neither read nor write very well. It was a fact he boasted about in the face of his enormous success. This lack of education however, did not detract from the man's innate savvy. He was a charmer and his rugged good looks had hardly paled with age. If the hair on his head and lip had not become so white then he might have defied his fifty-eight years by at least fifteen.

But like so many men it was his ego that made him foolish. But like so many men this was considered more a sign of confidence than vanity.

The disruptive influence of Anne Sutton on the de Beer household did not upset the mayor. He was only too happy to have his wife preoccupied with wasting his money rather than his time, and thought that what Miss Sutton lacked in compassion, she made up for with her eyes. They were beyond blue, they were violet. De Beer would sometimes stride right up to her, even in front of his wife, and in his Afrikaans accent declare that although she may have been christened Anne, she would always be Violet to him.

Thin, pale, humourless Anne Sutton was a virgin at twenty-seven and looked set to remain so. The eyes were the only remarkable thing in that otherwise tired little face. And yet her reaction to her employer's silly remarks was that of a woman so regularly pursued that she appeared more bored than thrown by his attentions and she'd respond in a weary tone saying that she was well aware of the colour of her eyes, all the time rolling the globes in question and hanging her head to one side, and then quite often suggest that the mayor being a man of some substance, focus his attention on more substantial matters. The scolded de Beer would roar with laughter and goad, "Exactly right Violet. Exactly!"

If Anne Sutton could have tipped Thys de Beer off a cliff as easily as she might have an old chest of drawers, she would have.

Quaint flirtatiousness was a Thys de Beer trademark. It was considered amusing by that society which so favoured his sex. They even turned a blind eye to his somewhat less quaint habit of frequenting of the local whorehouse. De Beer was quite open about his pursuit of pleasure at 7 Blunt Street and would even defend the habit publicly, saying how it was a far better thing for a man to pay for the service than to dally with another man's wife. The fact that he was also doing just that never deterred him from delivering the opinion, even when the wife in question and her husband were present.

For all its stuffy pretensions, there was a racy aspect to British conduct, which added an especially appealing dimension to the lives of a handful of Oudtshoorners rich enough to get away with it. They relished the hypocrisy. It was also a thrill to kick discreetly against the conservative Dutch Reformed Church. Not that any of them stopped attending Sunday worship, but that was where the hypocrisy came in handy.

Sara de Beer couldn't have cared less what her husband got up to. She had money, and status, and now, thanks to Anne Sutton's stately tips, she was about to have royalty.

The News

$\mathcal{S}$ara de Beer's husband was not only rich and powerful, more importantly to her he was usually the first person in Oudtshoorn to hear significant news. Thys knew his wife was silly, and true, the only sexual intercourse he'd had in nearly twenty years had been with another man's spouse or one of Rosie Botha's girls, but he retained an unwavering affection for his second bride nonetheless. She was idiotic, but, unlike his first wife, she was without malice and for that he thanked God every night before he settled down in his own four-poster.

As a mark of De Beer's appreciation, when any especially juicy news reached his large, brown ears first, he would leave his office directly and dart home to tell his Sara. (He avoided using the telephone on such occasions due to the eavesdropping of Nonnie van Tonder at the telephone exchange. When Nonnie discovered his trick she was outraged. "Me?! Listen in on calls?! I could sue him for that, for making me look unprofessional," she told her mother who told her that Esther Schultz had heard that De Beer had told his wife that he had heard that Nonnie was reluctant to get off the line. Nonnie learnt her legal jargon from listening in on calls she put through to Jonson and Abrahams Law Practitioners.)

The news that a prince was about to visit Oudtshoorn was perhaps the most thrilling example of this. "I'll never forget where I was when Thys told me the news," explained Sara to as many smart ladies as happened to cross her path the day the news came, "I was on the verandah!" And there the anecdote would end. No punch line, virtually mid-sentence. Frustrated listeners usually paused awkward-ly before trying to elicit a more satisfactory ending to the tale. "Yes? ...And what did he say? ...And what did you say?" they said.

At this Sara could never quite remember what her husband had said, but her own words she would never forget: "I said, 'Oh Thys, that is so exacting! What must I wore'?"

Sara de Beer wasn't the only person who found the news 'exact-ing' and a string of real English ladies not only cringed at possibly the best news told the dullest way they had ever heard, but they thought it exceedingly bad form for an Afrikaans couple to have been informed of the miracle before themselves. After all, it wasn't every day that a prince visited the Little Karoo!

News of the prince's visit broke in September, his arrival was expected in January, but a fever, sparked by the prospect, began to burn right away. Camps were formed, and rivalries that hadn't existed before promptly welled up and festered. Great friends became arch enemies and unexpected alliances were forged in reverse.

Everyone wanted a piece of the prince. Some even wanted to become a piece of the prince: *their* daughter would dance with him at the ball. *She* would of course enchant him. *He* would be *their* son-in-law. *Their* grandson would inherit the throne! Imaginations ran wild around a core of drab debutantes and a prince about whom they knew nothing other than that he was fascinatingly single.

Those without any daughters of marrying age squabbled over a thousand other things: who would host the ball? Who would make the speeches? Who would be introduced? Who would do the introduc-ing? Whose birds would be visited? Whose plumes would be presented? And on and on. Royalty became an obsession.

The Royal Committee

$\mathscr{L}$ady Agatha Teeling-Smith and Sara de Beer crossed paths more than the former would have liked though never quite often enough to satisfy the latter. There had been occasions when Sara's need to be near Agatha – who she believed actually secreted an essence of aristocracy so precious that a literal rubbing of shoulders could advance her own upliftment alchemically – spun out of control and she took to following her about the place. Agatha found the stalking most unpleasant and tried to prevent direct contact as much as possible. However, in a town the size of Oudtshoorn, approximation was often unavoidable, and the copious meetings held by Oudtshoorn's Official Royal Committee offered a perfect forum for Sara to try and acquire some of Agatha's potion.

The idea to form an official royal committee was that of Nessie Plaatjies. The excellent news about the visiting prince had reached Agatha – the same way it did so many others – by way of Sara de Beer.

The very same day the news arrived, Agatha was pondering a pair of daring mauve kid gloves in Hatfield's Department Store in a calm, contented manner when her meditation was shattered by 'that de Beer woman', who, from behind a rack of scarves standing to the extreme left of Agatha's line of vision, sprang forth with all the grace of something bovine attempting to hurdle a grid. "I'll never forget where I was when Thys told me the news!" she boomed oddly without so much as a greeting. "Good gracious woman! How frightful of you. A frailer woman than I might have lost her composure altogether and been thrust into an hypnotic state, never to return!" roared

Agatha, flapping the slivers of purple leather like a pair of mystical wings thereby adding drama to the expression of her displeasure. Sara, undeterred, moved over and pinched Agatha's arm, "I'm sorry, but you will understand me once I told to you the news!"

"What?" twitched Agatha. "What are you saying woman? I don't see what could possibly be important enough to justify this absurd approach," and she started inspecting the gloves at extremely close range whilst the jumping creature continued to deliver her garbled message.

The news so shocked Agatha that she found herself unable to fully respond. "Really," was all she could muster before asking the fascinated assistant behind the counter to kindly wrap the gloves and charge her account. She then turned and exited as if she had not seen Sara de Beer at all.

Agatha's shock propelled her home in record time. She needed to talk to Nessie at once. "Nessie!" called Agatha, the front door barely shut behind her. The tiny woman, who knew the full gamut of Madam's cries, almost dropped the glass she was drying and rushed to the hallway. Madam looked pale and was trembling slightly. But her voice had lost no vim. "Sherry, Nessie, sherry," she commanded as she made her way to her favourite chair in the drawing room where she subsided removing neither her hat nor her coat. Nessie hurried with the sherry and was beside her in a moment and only once Agatha had knocked back half a glass of the restorative liquid did she dare speak: "Madam gave me a hell of a fright. You mustn't do that. You know my heart is like a butterfly," and she tapped at her chest.

"*Your* heart! Pahf! If you could see *mine* right now it would make yours look like a dying moth in a saucer of milk." She downed the rest of the sherry and held out her glass for more. Nessie having predicted as much had the bottle to hand and swiftly obliged.

"Do you know what that dreadful Sara de Beer just had the temerity to tell me?" Nessie said nothing, just wore an expression that might have been taken for someone who has never known anything at all, a cunning affectation which generally resulted in her milking the speaker for everything they knew. "She accosted me in Hatfield's," continued Agatha "Leapt out from behind a rack of scarves like a tiger that has been shot in the rump, and proceeded to tell me, in the most tedious, most roundabout fashion, that in about six months time, Oudtshoorn is to be visited by ROY-AL-TY!"

Nessie was so amazed she took a swig of sherry straight from the bottle. Agatha, who had been staring ahead of her as she spoke, did not appear to notice, she just finished up her own drink then turned to Nessie for comment. "Well woman? Cat got your tongue?"

"Jeez I wouldn't be surprised if it did."

Nessie Plaatjies had witnessed the stalking of her madam by Thys de Beer's wife on several occasions, and nurtured a loathing of the mayor's wife as a result. She would often spot the stalker before Agatha did and was quick to hatch plans to help them dodge the fiend. Once when it looked like they had no option but to walk right into Sara on Main Street, she threw herself in front of a car in order to effect a distraction. (The road was wide and the vehicle slow, and six eggs from her basket were the only things that broke.)

Now Nessie fell into deep contemplation. Agatha eyed her maid briefly. "Well, what do you have to say to that?" she asked impatiently after a weighty five seconds had passed. Nessie stared ahead five more ticks of the mantel clock more before saying in a loud, spitty, conspiratorial whisper: "You must form a committee. A royal committee where you the boss and you decide what happens when the royal person comes." Much as Agatha adored the idea, it made her self-conscious. "But my dear, I can hardly appoint myself chairlady."

"You won't have to, you just call a meeting, say there must be a committee, and all that, to make sure everything is nice for the prince, and then make sure that they all understand that whoever is the boss must be a royal type of person. And that's you! You a Lady! Lady Agatha Teeling-Smith. They have to vote you, because it's the rules. Then you must just pull your face like so when you win," Nessie hitched her face into an expression of severest surprise.

And so of the one truly official royal committee Agatha Teeling-Smith was the chair, and Sara de Beer made it her business to make Thys de Beer make it his business to persuade the leader to find some special role for his adorable wife to play in the royal charade. One of de Beer's favourite business tactics was blatant bribery. It had generally served him well and always having been on reasonable terms with Lady Agatha he saw no reason why he should not try this method on her.

Agatha had been away from the safe confines of her family home too many years to be shocked by the approach, but the booty – birds, cash, even a bracelet dropped clumsily into her glass of wine at a dinner party – was not interesting enough to persuade her that Sara de Beer should be allowed to come within forty feet of the prince, let alone sit next to him at the royal banquet or have him to stay.

But Sara's desperation had infected her husband and Agatha's unwillingness to do as he asked made him embark on a course of action that he would one day regret.

Blackmail

Agatha's husband had loved his wife in a very special way. But he had also loved another in a different kind of special way. She was a rather ordinary young widow named Emma Wilmot. Agatha had discovered the affair within months of its commencement, but by then the lover was pregnant and walking away would not be so graceful.

After an initial burst of spite which had Agatha send several of Humphrey's best fossils off to be scattered somewhere desolate by one of her gardeners, she decided to help her husband sort out the mess he had made for himself, herself, and young Emma. Her suggestion that the woman, being virtually destitute, could be persuaded to leave the region forever and never reveal the identity of her child's father in exchange for a comfortable monthly allowance was tried and after some persuading (and the promise of occasional covert visits by her lover) it worked.

The woman left. The payments were made. All was well. However, once Humphrey died, Agatha, devastated and depressed as she was, experienced another surge of loathing and stopped the allowance at once. Sixteen years later, the destitute orphan of Lord Humphrey Teeling-Smith found herself employment at Rosie Botha's house of fun.

Thys de Beer discovered the delicious gossip during what started out as a rather woeful visit to 'the girls'. Primrose – that was the child's name – had been his choice that evening and she had only to ask "What's the matter Mayor?" once for him to launch into a woeful monologue about that "damn, bloody-minded" Agatha Teeling-Smith and her reluctance to co-operate on the matter of his wife and the pending prince. Primrose listened to the whole complaint before asking him to repeat the damn woman's name. Then it was Thys de Beer's turn to shut up and listen. When he heard Primrose's story he had never minded shutting his own gob less.

Just as her mother had been persuaded into silence, Thys de Beer now curbed Primrose. "Now listen Primrose," he said, swatting her tiny hands away from his groin. "Listen to me. You know I am the most powerful man in Oudtshoorn don't you? Well I can make things nice for you if you do as I say." After all, what good would it be to him if she got to Agatha first?

After a particularly tense meeting of the Official Royal Committee, during which Sara de Beer suggested that she and a group of small dancing girls should dress as fairies and surprise the prince by linking hands and surrounding him at some point during the proceedings thereby enchanting him with their charismatic twirling, the mayor offered Agatha his arm and insisted on walking her home. After some protest from the lady he was able to wave his carriage away and make the journey towards her house quickly on foot – just the way she liked it.

Anyone watching the grand pair striding boldly up the main street towards Agatha's house would have known the precise moment things took a turn for the worse, for they stopped dead. Agatha, incapable of losing her composure, lost instead control of her jaw and it ground quickly at her gloating escort: "I am hardly surprised by your vile little tactic," she said then ground some more before continuing: "Very well. Your terrible little wife is welcome to make as much of a fool of herself as she likes when the prince comes. You make a list of demands and I'll agree to them. See if I care." Then she continued briskly to her home alone.

Inside her front door she shooed a waiting Nessie Plaatjies away. That night there was nothing she wished to discuss.

The Others

The idea of a visiting prince thrilled more than those who thought that they or their kin might marry one. People who hardly knew what royalty was started to buzz once they'd had it explained to them. It was as if such a visit would somehow change their lives: a prince would have been transported along the track, and playing, drinking, fighting and fornicating on the lines would never be the same again. From the train's window, a prince would have seen their dust, their mountains, their homes, perhaps even themselves. They would truly exist after the prince had passed.

Sloth and Cruelty

Seven years had elapsed since Van der Want and his mad battered Erma settled seventy-five miles east of Oudtshoorn. In that time they had built a hovel, spawned three boys and made a small fortune out of eighty birds. Erma had nursed a hundred bruises and wept a million tears. The unhappy home stood with the start of the great mountain slopes a hundred yards to the rear, and a railway siding a hundred yards in front. The house itself was a temple of gloom. Two dark, low-ceilinged rooms made of mud that always smelled of smoke were kept as clean as possible by the neat Erma, despite the mess deliberately made by her husband who would throw food on the floor, never empty his own pot of shit, and keep sick animals inside. Van der Want owned three thousand hectares of land and was lord to four families of poor whites and fifteen even poorer families of colour.

When police chief Frik Hanekom identified Van der Want as perfect proxy for duties he was too lazy to carry out himself in the Vlakteplaas district, it was a start of a great new terror.

Hannekom was a brutal man. Physically he was just as repulsive as Van der Want, but in quite the opposite way. He was short, perhaps five foot six, and his thinning hair was the colour of sand. His small stumpy teeth appeared chiselled into spikes making his purple beer-bloated face all the meaner. His voice was high-pitched and his speech was hurried, almost excitable. Spittle gathered at the corners of his mouth as he spoke and his short bluish tongue flicked in and out of the slimy hole whenever he paused in conversation, at which point he'd breathe out heavily and shower anybody too close with yellow gob, making a sound like "BLEARTH".

Thanks to the extensive powers bestowed upon him by his drinking companion Judge Bull of Uniondale, Frik's lust for instilling fear and administering torture found a pragmatic outlet. He believed God had sent the Afrikaners to tame Africa just as he had sent Jesus Christ to curb the Jews, and the punishments he devised to fulfil this holy task were merciless. But Frik struggled to mete out foul punishment evenly across the vast area he was employed to oversee. He was sadistic, but he was lazy. So he rode through the countryside, looking out for bad reputations in search of a suitable stand-in for part of the region. A man who would require no more payment than odious gratification as remuneration for his help.

Van der Want was not used to visitors and could not shift the resentment he felt at being invaded now. Hanekom sized up the big man well and set about apologising for the intrusion: "Very irritating being disturbed …Know the feeling …Hate visitors myself …Most people aren't worth the effort …May I sit?"

Van der Want was already seated. As none of his other family members were allowed to occupy the small dirt veranda, there were no seats, other than a crate Van der Want used to rest his feet on. Hanekom pawed the box towards himself and squatted opposite his host. The seat was unsteady and the law man had been offered nothing to drink. Normally he would have considered this an affront and allowed his displeasure to show, but now a combination of fear and desire kept temper at bay. The look of the mephitic man he had heard such news of frightened him, a fact that impressed him enormously, and the dead taste in his parched mouth had a perverse smack of pleasure about it. Van der Want said nothing, just chewed on his pipe. Hanekom continued: "I'm sure you know better than most what people are," he said. "Scratch the surface and they will lie, and steal, and break the law for the fun of it. Laughing at the farmers who keep them alive. Laughing at the police. Laughing at God. My good friend Judge Bull of Uniondale and I have been working to try and bring some order to the area. But we don't have enough men to clamp down the way we would like to." He paused. Van der Want waited.

"Mr Van der Want, I'd like to ask you a question. What would you do if you caught a thief on your farm? Maybe one of your workers, stealing milk and butter? What would you do? You've been good to the man. Given him and his family work when they turned up here half starved and begged you to help them. Then you start to notice things missing. First eggs then milk and butter. What do you do about it? Eh?" Frik went "BLERTH" and waited for Van der Want's response. Van der Want began to smile, his two fat lips stretched tighter across his teeth. "They would never dare do that here," came his eventual reply, which satisfied Frik Hanekom that Van der Want would indeed be the cruellest man for the job.

Hanekom stayed a few minutes more, explaining how, if Van der Want accepted the responsibility, he would not be interfered with. How he would be trusted as the strong arm of the law in the region. Then he apologised for the fact that there was to be no payment, shook the giant's hand and left.

Van der Want's sons who had been spying on the scene from the shed, trembled as they watched the short man ride away. They had only ever seen their father show his teeth that way when he was about to slap them or Ma and they wondered why he had not punched the intruder. That afternoon nobody got hurt, but the real pain at Vlakteplaas was about to begin. And as the lazy policeman made his way back over the hills, he dragged a veil darker than any even he could have imagined, across the land in his wake.

A man caught trying to steal a cow was forced to watch while his four-year-old son was tied to the tail of an ox and kicked to death.

A woman who had pissed in a churn of milk to avenge herself on the farmer to whom it belonged, was held down while Van der Want's pet hawk pecked viciously at grain he'd inserted into her vagina.

A labourer accused of stirring up protest amongst his fellow workers had a hole punched through his tongue.

Houses

*B*eneficiaries of the second feather boom, desperate to spend as much money as they could, took to building houses. Proper houses. Building was an extravagant though convenient process. Men in neat, pressed pin-striped trousers talked buyers through a detailed catalogue of illustrated options and, for a small fortune, clients could order from a variety of miniature Victorian mansions, with fittings and furniture to match, to be shipped from England and erected on site. A glorious age of prefabrication was begun, and the houses known as feather palaces grew up out of the ground, right next to the small, crude, mud-rock homes of before. But for some of the more timid folk who had plucked a better life for themselves it was all too much. Lomin and Annelisa Olins were a case in point.

The decision to engage the process in the first place had been made gaily after Lomin had enjoyed a particularly profitable day at the feather market and had been persuaded to celebrate by way of a few ales with a handful of his fellow lucksters.

Two members of the party had already embarked on the process of palace building and were keen to describe it as painless and not nearly as difficult as being dragged to town by their wives and forced to shop for clothing at Hatfield's department store.

Eventually, when one said, "And the funny part is that those smart guys with all the books seem to know what you want before you do," and when another confirmed that this was true, Lomin Olins, who was not much used to liquor and needed more than just moral support that day, made his way to the office of the Oudtshoorn Housing

Company and allowed one of the smart gentlemen there to pick out a home with all its trimmings for him.

Less than a year later, not twenty yards from their gritty little cottage, stood the Olins' very own feather palace. A tension gripped the family of eight as the finishing touches and final furnishings were placed in the new home. Annelisa decided it was a bad idea for the family to set foot inside in case they upset the process. Lomin agreed. And so they observed from a safe distance instead. When the last workmen rode away, Mr Trott of the pin-striped trousers appeared on the veranda looking bewildered. "Mr Olins," he called to the tallest of the ragged figures who stood in a row staring open-mouthed in his direction as if the stoep were a stage and he the only player, "Is anything the matter?" Olins walked slowly over and mounted the boards. "I need you to sign, to confirm that all you have ordered and paid for is in order," said the salesman and moved to enter the house. Olins did not budge. "We have to check the inventory to make sure that it is to your satisfaction." Olins remained still, then called to his wife to join him before following Trott inside.

Slowly the owners of the brand new house began to smile and even sit briefly on a chair or open a cutlery drawer. They were so distracted by the finery that they paid little attention to the inventory call and the husband scratched a mark in Trott's book and the man of clothes took his leave. Then, with hardly a word Annelisa ushered Lomin back out the same way they had entered and locked the door behind them.

Later that day Annelisa re-entered the home with her eldest daughter Magda armed with sheets for covering the new lounge suite. (At church she had heard of wealthy people doing such things.) At dinner that night in the old house no mention was made of the new, and the slurping of soup could be heard unfuzzed by chatter.

The family never did make the twenty yard leap and live in the new house. It was being kept nice and new for when they had fancy visitors, like Dominee Coetzee. But he only came once.

About eighteen months into the building craze, Van der Want got wind of it from train driver Ben Isaac.

Isaac was a Jew who came from a long line of teachers, but he was no scholar. He nurtured just one ambition: to sit at the helm of a great, steaming locomotive. To Ben that was the most glamourous thing in the world.

He realised his dream at the age of thirty-eight, after spending twenty years unhappily lugging props about Port Elizabeth's Victory Theatre. His naturally nervous disposition was quite unsuited to accommodating volatile thespian tempers, easily triggered by a tilted sunset or jerkily drawn curtain. The end came the evening the Port Elizabeth players found themselves felled by a ten foot high muslin oak just as they were about to witness some especially riveting petulance from Hamlet himself. The recriminations were too much for the jumpy stage hand to bear, and he hurried out into the night, wet with tears, never to return.

Ben Isaac's railway job was like a mask which shielded his vulnerable character from the things that would otherwise make him shake. Encased in an inch of black cast iron, in control of hundreds of tons of movement he was safe. Whilst working, or talking about his job, Ben was as steady as the engine he controlled, and, unlike the rest who said a prayer when the monster passed, he spoke freely to Van der Want on his stops at the Vlakteplaas siding.

"Oh yes, these houses, palaces really, are popping up all over the place," Ben called casually from the safety of the sooty shunter. Van der Want felt his guts twinge with a mixture of interest and jealousy: was he not the richest man in the valley? Was he not the strong arm of the law? Did he not also deserve to live in a palace? Yes! He wanted one too. But he wasn't about to venture into Oudtshoorn in order to see some catalogue, and he didn't want any men in neat pinstriped trousers visiting Vlakteplaas either. Instead, he hired Duppie du Plessis.

Duppie du Plessis had led a luckless life. As a boy he was the only one ever caught stealing gob stoppers at Potter's General Store. He was the one still undecided about which direction to run in whenever a ball had smashed through a window. He was the one kept out of secrets that later some irate adult would question him about, periodically cuffing him because he was unable to reveal the truth. His bad luck made him a target for all to bully and all to blame. Adulthood didn't change things much, and Duppie was never able to get away with the normal wrongdoings most people take for granted as necessary sins. Even his attempts at practical joking flopped. And yet he showed a genuine degree of surprise each time misfortune struck. The reek of failure emanated from Duppie du Plessis in pungent essence form.

Duppie had learned the building trade from his father but when the old man died, being incapable of running the business himself, he soon frittered away his small inheritance and settled for labouring for another. It was his love of liquor that deemed it necessary for him to steal timber and fittings from a site one time, and for this he was promptly hindered and arrested. It was a time of unkind legal practice in the wilderness, and sentencing for most offences was left to the whim of the magistrate on duty. These barbaric men of justice favoured punishments with dramatic biblical emphasis. Flogging, starvation, confiscation of livestock, and banishment were all popular options. The court offered Duppie a choice; one year in prison or five in exile. The guilty opted for the latter, but soon decided that the judge must have had some clairvoyant insight into the building industry outside the Oudtshoorn district, for it hardly existed. Remote farmers either lacked the money or the pretensions for wasting money on fancy homes. So Duppie and his wife Clara factotumed their way about the countryside for whatever they could get.

Like many other long distance messages, the one from Van der Want to Du Plessis was conveyed along the track by way of Ben Isaac who had suggested the match. When the news reached the destitute builder at his tent near the track twenty miles west of Vlakteplaas, he and his wife were on the verge of starvation.

"… Yes, so it's a serious job then you know. You'd better get to see him as quick as you can, before he finds someone else you know. Just follow the track like I said." And with these words Ben started moving the pitch bulk away. Duppie fell to his knees as soon as he realised what it was Ben Isaac was telling him, and started to sob. "O God," he yelped, "Oh God fank you. I know I am useless, like somefink you frew away … Oh God! Fank you Lord Jesus. I promise …" at this point, too moved to continue he flopped face first into the scrub and wailed. His wife, who had heard the whole thing watched passively beside him. Then, without moving her eyes from the spectacle, she hitched her skirt and crouched to pee.

Duppie had never heard of Van der Want, and Van der Want had only heard of Duppie through Ben Isaac, which was as well for both men.

Mares and Lists and Orders

Duppie had eaten the mangy mare that had been his only asset and sole form of transportation just two months into exile, and so for the trip to Vlakteplaas he borrowed a neighbour's donkey which wasn't easy because the neighbour remembered what had happened to Duppie's mare and feared that the builder would snack on his own beast before the trip was done. Eventually a deal was struck and Duppie exchanged his betrothed for the ass and agreed that should he fail to return the donkey within a week then the neighbour could keep the wife.

Two days later Duppie had hugged the track all the way to the Vlakteplaas siding. The heat was almost audible and the black letters on the white sign appeared at first through a mirage. Once they became clear Duppie felt that twinge of pride he always did when it was confirmed he could still read. He arrived at four in the afternoon. It was eerily quiet once the donkey stood still. Duppie looked up at Van der Want's house. A fly darted, loud as a trumpet, around his large, raw, peeling nose. His tongue was dry and swollen. His arse itched. He dismounted and led the donkey up the slope and round the back to the kitchen door. On the dirt in the shade of the kitchen wall, Duppie saw a clump of hair, a plait of grass and some chicken livers inside a circle of beans – Erma's crazy magic stuff. He stood staring a moment before someone hit his head hard from behind.

Erma knew nothing about her husband's arrangement with Duppie. She bent over the stinking body as it moved slowly, grizzling and spitting. "I'm here for Van der Want!" Duppie yelled, "I'm the builder!" Then she hit him three more times with the broom she was holding, moved inside the kitchen and slammed the door.

It was almost dark when Van der Want arrived home, his sons behind him in a cart pulled by four mules who looked like they could have eaten Duppie and his donkey if they had the energy. Duppie had found some water and was slouched next to a gangly nasturtium bush he'd been steadily plucking at and munching on for over an hour. Erma had forgotten the stranger almost as soon as she'd whacked him and was back inside the kitchen clenching her jaw and crushing corn and meditating on the pain in her teeth.

Duppie stood and waited as Van der Want made his way past him to the house. An emerald stalk still hanging from the corner of his mouth, he made to speak but Van der Want turned just then and signalled to him to stay put and entered the house.

The master emerged moments later carrying a jug of beer and two glasses. Unaccustomed as he was to engaging others, Van der Want's language was gruff and unclear. "I want a house. A palace this stupid bloody town people call it. Big ... but better ... better and big with everything around like this," he made a dabbing gesture up and down with one of his great fleshy hands in the direction of his two roomed shack. "And with this thing for sitting on the front. But big ... and stairs and everything ... and with steps ... and with glass."

Duppie said: "Eh... Eh... Eh–he... Eh... Eh... Eh... Eh... E," and nodded vigorously. His cheeks pulled back into the shape of unquestioning assent though he wasn't clear on any of what he was being told. But he knew that the palaces only came in a few varieties and he was confident that all he had to do was find one, sketch it, order materials, arrange delivery to the Vlakteplaas siding, and then build the thing. It was no small task, but as his only other option was starvation, he jabbered on about how it would be as easy as beating your wife on a Monday and Van der Want surprised himself when he laughed at the saying. Duppie was unaware of just how rare the sound of Van der Want's laughter was but he felt relieved to have impressed him nonetheless and kept repeating it over and over and over "Beating your wife on a Monday. Easy as that." Then he collapsed.

Revived with rusks and coffee, but with no offer of overnight accommodation to prepare him for the fifteen hour trek towards Oudtshoorn, Duppie started back. As he slept alongside the track that night, he dreamed of food. When he awoke he eyed the donkey hungrily and considered sacrificing the wife. But some latent affection for the woman who had stood by him through all his woes prevailed. Besides, it seemed that the Van der Want commission was going to snatch them back from the brink of oblivion after all and he might once more have a house of his own for the woman to clean. Holding this merry thought all the way home, when he reached his Clara, he couldn't help kissing her.

The advance from Van der Want enabled Duppie to buy a mule. The builder, his wife and their new asset walked forty-five miles towards Oudtshoorn, then, with the town visible in the distance, Duppie, too afraid to advance any closer, pushed his long-suffering spouse up onto the animal's back and dispatched her to fetch pencils and paper for sketching.

The fear of being caught copying a nice house within the Oudtshoorn district proved to be more paranoia on Duppie's part than anything else. Nobody knew or cared who he was, and he needn't have gone to the trouble of squatting quietly at dusk with a dozen twigs stuck in his hat for camouflage as he drew.

The house he chose to copy was a fairly simple affair. A white-washed rectangle with five sash windows along the front, shutters and a double fronted door with blue and red stained glass surround. A narrow verandah ran along the facade. A zinc roof with an attic inside, as evidenced by two tiny mansards jutting out, and a restrained wrought iron, broekielace frill along the top edge.

The example was built on flat ground, but in a flush of creativity, Duppie, remembering the sloped location of Van der Want's farm, decided that half a dozen steps leading up to the front porch would add grandeur to the dwelling, and these he sketched in without any reference at all.

Choosing and ordering the right cornicing, pressed ceilings, doors, panelling and other interior embellishments was tricky, especially as Duppie was too afraid to enter the forbidden city himself. If the order was wrong and any of Van der Want's money wasted, then, the boss had assured him, he would wish he had starved to death in the dust with his beaten wife. There was no need for Van der Want to spell out exactly what he would do to Duppie; the face that had laughed only moments before was enough to haunt his sleep most nights. Sometimes he even thought he saw Van der Want when he was awake, a bird's shadow, a rustle in the grass, a passing voice deepened by distance, and Duppie would have to strain not to piss his pants with fright. But with Van der Want's money in hand he had no choice. He sent his wife to the hardware merchant with a list of descriptions and measurements and hoped for the best.

Clara was not the dunce Duppie assumed her to be. She never spoke, she was born mute, but she was no dummy and finally proved as much by succeeding brilliantly at the task. She wasn't even tempted to steal any of the money. Her mouth was impaired but there was nothing wrong with her ears and she had heard about the brute at Vlakteplaas. The ordering took a week to complete and on one of her errands into town she wrangled herself a job in the kitchen at the Queen's Hotel so she delivered the last of the lists to her husband – which were now all signed by whatever merchants she had visited: 'order filled as written' – then, without dismounting from the mule, she turned one hundred and eighty degrees and cantered back to town for good. Duppie was left standing nowhere, clutching pencils and papers and a bottle of water. He yelled and pounded the ground, forgetting his resolve to remain unnoticed in the district. But barred from following her, he never saw that "dumb-stupid-bastard-bitch-shitty-whore-wife" of his again.

The wait for the goods on order to arrive was a painful one. Six months it took, with Duppie skulking about Van der Want's place, begging more food than he should, trying Van der Want's hospitality (he was allowed a corner of the goat barn to sleep in). But once the deliveries started arriving, the runaway wife's shopping success was clearly apparent.

Mostly things went smoothly. Duppie was hopeless at lots in life but he had a knack for measurements, which was an excellent thing for a builder with only remote access to building materials. Of course there were hitches. But fortunately, it was always Kolo's fault.

"No man ... shit ... okay. Kolo!" Duppie called impatiently to Kolo, a labourer Van der Want had loaned him. Kolo wasn't very bright. Dimwitted in fact. Duppie exploited this, using him as a vent for his own cerebral limitations which was a luxury he had never known on a building site before – himself usually being the one cuffed about the head by some irate foreman, and it was something he enjoyed immensely.

Duppie stood on a crate at a doorway which had a fanlight frame at the top made to hold a piece of glass exactly thirty-six by twenty-four inches. He was hot and exasperated, a piece of glass twenty-four by twenty-six inches in his hands. "Kolo come here. Come!" Duppie puffed impatiently. The labourer came over, a large chunk of dried mortar stuck in his hair, holding a brick in his left hand and a trowel in his right. "Look at dis." Duppie demonstrated the mistake in size by moving the glass easily from side to side in the frame. "Look at dis fing now. It's not right. It's too small. Now what am I supposed to do about dat, hey?" Sweat stung Duppie's eyes. He climbed down and jerked his head first towards the glass, then the doorway. Then the glass, then the doorway. He did this energetically several times. Kolo watched the door frame as though he thought it might walk off, his mouth hung open and he didn't seem to notice the sweat that blurred his vision.

"De bloody glass is too small man Kolo. So what am I supposed to do wiv de bloody fing now? Eh?" Kolo looked at the glass and shook his head to show that he understood something was wrong, which was all he could seem to manage. Duppie lay the glass on the ground and tutted at it a bit, then turned to look up at the doorframe one more time. There he saw Kolo climbing the ladder and placing the brick he was holding inside the fanlight frame. He then hopped back down, fetched the pane of glass, climbed back up and held it next to the brick in the hole. "Are you stupid?" said Duppie realising it was a far better idea than any he had had, "You must cut de bricks den put one eiver side of the glass so dat de glass is in de middle." He forced Kolo off the ladder and took over.

And so it went: mansards but no attic; broekielace decoration that stopped before the corner of the veranda; slanting floors propped to a better angle using sheep bones and old tobacco tins; a roof crowned with two upside down chimney pots.

Building took eighteen months to complete. When it was done Van der Want was bowled over by the five-roomed mansion. Once most of the structure was in place, he flashed those awful teeth at Duppie more than once and nodded approval. When it was finished, Van der Want dragged a huge, molting armchair onto the verandah, and there he roosted endlessly, a rifle resting in his lap, surveying the district. From that slightly elevated position never again would a soul move about that valley without the eye of Van der Want falling upon them like a curse.

Who's the King?

$\mathcal{E}$ight years into the second feather boom, Van der Want had been at Vlakteplaas fifteen joyless summers. He had been the unofficial arm of the law for seven of those years. His sons, thirteen, eleven and ten years old, were as obedient as any father could have wished, and his wife grew steadily more nervous around him. Few newcomers had settled in the area and those who did were generally employed by Van der Want. They were his subjects and existed at his mercy.

The new house further boosted Van der Want's belief in his own supremacy. Even when he heard that a prince was expected to come along the track he did not flinch. "Yes, it will be a wonderful thing for the region you know," said Ben Isaac. "A real prince. All the money in the world and lots of gold on his clothes and, and, and lots of gold in his bank I should think!" Who was this prince anyway, thought Van der Want. And what did he care about a prince when he was king at Vlakteplaas?

The Elands

Thomas Eland was a kind, puckered, humble bag of bones. He had had three younger sisters, but only one survived childhood. The Elands were poor farm labourers, but their predicament hadn't made them drunk or cruel. They believed that Jesus was their saviour, although it seemed that they might have to die in order to elicit his sympathy.

Thomas's parents worked for a struggling farmer named Abel Lategan. He mostly paid them in amounts of food whenever he could, but when there was hardly enough to feed his own progeny, the Elands went without.

Simon Eland, the father, could not read, but Mina Eland, the mother, could. She had been taught how by Abel Lategan's late mother, a fine old woman who dedicated three afternoons a week to teaching her labourer's children. The lessons stopped when her husband died. Old Reenen Lategan left her so much gambling debt to pay that she was no longer afforded the luxury of time and she and her four sons had to start farming all over again. Three years later only Abel remained at Mooiplaas. One brother drowned during a flood, two others moved to Port Elizabeth seeking easier livelihoods: one in a bakery, one in a bar.

But by the time her lessons stopped, Mina had already learned what could not be unlearned, her *abc* and *def* and so on, and she would scratch her thoughts into the sand and read them back to herself for practice.

Ma Eland made sure that an hour each evening was devoted to the task of sharing her gift with her two remaining children. The three would huddle around two candles, squinting at the only book in the house, anxious to read God's stories because that way they could hear His voice whenever they pleased, not just on Sundays.

The evening lesson was a gentle ritual which included Pa, who, although he could never get the hang of the letters himself, was awestruck rather than embittered by the regret.

With small, grey supper eaten more quickly than would have been comfortable had the portions ever been anything more than meagre, Pa would rise from the table and fetch the Bible down from the short yellow shelf above the front door. He would carefully brush away whatever dust had settled on the cover since the night before, then make his way deftly across the tiny room to where his darling was waiting, a painfully thin child crouched at each elbow, eagerly await-ing enlightenment. Ma would thank Pa as she took the tutor from his calloused, brown hand, deliberately making contact with the horny skin as she did so, and then begin.

But reading set Ruth and Thomas apart from the other labourers in spirit only, for their skill was bound in leather too dark for desk work.

When their parents died, Ruth and Thomas, knotted together with tough, wiry strands of love and hunger, made a pact never to leave one another. It was love that finally did divide them.

When she was thirty-two years old, Ruth met Hannes Willemse, a blacksmith's assistant who had lost his job in Oudtshoorn after an argument with his boss about some or other small thing that was soon forgotten and made not much sense at all, but ruined his life anyway. He left town in search of another master and he asked for work at Lategan's farm, but there was none. There was only Ruth.

The first time Hannes glimpsed his precious, she was trudging across the veld towards him, dragging a huge sack of firewood behind her. It was late afternoon and she'd been doing the work of two mules since sun up. Her face was shiny with sweat and the grubby red scarf around her head looked ready to slip right off the back of her skull. There wasn't an ounce of fat on her, but labour had made her body strong and the muscles in her arms were exquisitely etched.

Hannes rushed to help her. He introduced himself shyly, then when she didn't volunteer it, he asked her name. Ruth watched the stranger closely, trying to surmise his motives. Rape out there in the veld was not uncommon. But she liked the man's sad, fleshy face, which was beginning to droop around the jowls and spoke: "I'm Ruth," she said.

Hannes was suspended in contemplation of her beauty. Never before had he seen such a woman. The colour of her skin, rich, burnt ochre, kept soft with pig fat which she rubbed into it every morning and every night. And her eyes, well they were like chinks of pale jade. Hannes felt himself falling in love. They were married three weeks later.

Four months after the wedding, Ruth's brother was resting in the shade of a large, scrubby bush on his three mile walk home from church, when he became a stumbling block for a drunkard named Mary Wessels. Thomas, startled by the clash, quickly sat up and stared amazed at the soggy wretch who had tripped over him and now lay cursing at his side. "You stupid bloody bugger! My fucking leg! Aaaah!"

It was a terrible sound. It was terrible and blasphemous, and at first Thomas was too shocked to know what to do. Then suddenly he felt a message from heaven come to him, straight through his eyebrows. It travelled down each fine, black hair, through the follicle and straight into the frontal lobes of his brain: he must save this poor young woman. He must!

Thomas Eland was forty-one when he married twenty-four year old Mary.

At first the new loyalties did not separate the siblings. The Eland shack was simply inhabited by four again instead of two. But they were worse off than before. Hannes seemed unable to find more than one day of paid work a week, and Mary, who had hardly worked an hour in her life, continued in that vein. But Ruth and Thomas were used to the hollow feeling in their bellies by then and hardly noticed it any more. The trouble was with Mary.

Mary would find the Lord through the gentle coaxing of her husband one day, and find a bottle of liquor the next, usually a reward from a passing letch. Thomas often found his wife being humped by a stranger. He would sometimes try to pull Mary out from under the man, other times he would just shake his head and leave the house. Mary had usually drunk enough liquor by then to release her grip on the man without too much fuss, but if she hadn't been paid by the time Thomas intervened she would bite and claw at husband and customer alike, and scream like a fox until she was handed a bottle.

Occasionally one of the men would fight back, throw a few punches at Thomas and the whore who hadn't given him what he'd come for, but usually they understood the routine as being part of the bargain that was Mary, and eventually moved off into veld with their pants half undone.

Ruth shared her brother's gift of tolerance, and although she did not like her sister-in-law she respected her brother's noble motives and rarely said what she thought.

When Mary was sober and feeling faithful she wouldn't hesitate to cast aspersions on the lack of God she sensed in others. In her game of absolutes, Hannes was her favourite, if unwilling opponent. "When did you last go to church Hannes Willemse? Hey?" she'd demand, shoving an accusing finger into the gut of the man with the sad eyes.

Hannes would grab his hat as soon as she started, and leave the house in search of Ruth. But the demented banshee would follow a while, waving Thomas's mother's precious Bible above her head: "Do you even know your scriptures?! You're the devil's own child Hannes Willemse, and you never going to be saved like me!"

Hannes dreaded Mary's other extreme even more. Drunk, she

would push herself down on her brother-in-law's lap, rubbing her chest in his face. "Do you like my titties? Hey Hannes? Do you want to suck them like a baby?" Hannes would flick her to the floor and run to Ruth in search of goodness. But a sense of hopelessness welled inside him and he began to keep a small bottle of liquor, which he topped up at the expense of Mary's visitors. Just as semi-comatose passion was reaching its vociferous peak he'd sneak a little of the booty into a bottle of his own and slip away to drink.

The habit was almost dreamlike to Hannes. It felt like someone else stole the alcohol. Someone else drank it. Someone else enjoyed the temporary sense of relief which the drinking brought to his heart. Ruth had whiffed it but couldn't bring herself to accuse or question. She just cried sometimes when she was out on the farm, where only the cattle heard her and they didn't care.

Hannes lay on the floor near the hearth, staring up at the ceiling of soot. He was numbed by the moonshine he had pilfered the day before. "Can you see heaven Hannes Willemse?" He could make out Mary, swaying unsteadily over him, one foot either side of his head. She was naked and stretching her labia as far apart as she could. Her face was beginning to dehydrate into skinny creases because of the drink, but her body was still smooth, youthful, firm.

The fecund sex was too strong to wash away, and that night, when Ruth climbed into bed behind her love, it smothered her. The next morning before the sun had fully hauled itself up onto the horizon, Ruth gripped her brother as hard as she could, then released him suddenly and headed off into the unknown with her man.

De Rust

$\mathcal{T}$he Lategan farm was near the village of De Rust, about thirty miles east of Oudtshoorn. It was a runt of a village. One church, one shop, a scattering of farms. But the community was close and not awed by their rich neighbours. It was a place on its own route to a different part of heaven.

Like a lot of other places which had names and not much else, De Rust's stretch of railway track was the focus of much activity. There was a small market behind the tin siding and next to that a shop that sold everything from soap to sausages. Traders parked their wagons in the shade cast by two big poplar trees that grew nearby, and drinking was done either outside the shop that sold everything or on the track itself.

The station was sixty feet of platform, four feet high and five feet wide, with a whitewashed wooden sign with 'De Rust' painted in black letters on either side. Passengers rarely got on or off the train at that sign and the thundering locomotive would toot and slow down but never stop there unless someone was jumping about with their arms in the air indicating that there was in fact something to send along the rails.

Whenever the engine did squeal to a halt, the driver would usually have some piece of news or hearsay to impart about happenings elsewhere along the line, and there was always a handful of locals willing to tolerate the lingering steam and listen.

It was Ben Isaac who had the pleasure of bringing the De Rusters news of the royal visit. The locals may on occasion have married those too closely related to themselves, but they knew what a prince was. It was all the fame and fortune in the world, and it was coming down the track to De Rust.

"No, well, I don't think he's stopping here, " said Ben quickly realising the misapprehension, "Just going past, you know. Just passing through – to Oudtshoorn, you know. "

The fancy ways of Oudtshoorn were not the ways of De Rust, even among the residents who did have money. Karel Prinsloo was a fine example of just that. To him, Oudtshoorners were just a bunch of snobs. A waste of space. "That's just bloody stupid," he said when he heard the news. Karel was the most vehement objector to the idea that the prince would just pass them by. A huge red-faced man, with an orange beard and a battered green fedora which he hardly ever pulled off his thick ginger curls, Karel owned the shop that sold everything and had also made a fair deal of money out of plumes. Apart from the obligatory drinking of hefty quantities of brandy, smoking was his only vice, and his cob pipe was as permanent a fixture in that great sun of a head as his hat. Now he raised his brows and pursed his lips and made as if delicately taking a sip of tea: "Would you like a cup of tea your Majesty?" Then lunging forward, shouting roughly, and making a punching motion like a left fist he added: "I'll take their tea and shove it up that stupid bloody mayor's backside!" His cronies laughed and Karel looked round at them excitedly. "Who is coming with me to take that bastard de Beer down a peg or two?!" he shouted. His cronies roared "Yes!". Ben Isaac who witnessed the scene felt like he might start to cry and pulled away before Morné Uys had finished loading his corn, forcing him to leap from the locomotive and spill.

"They're not in England now, " Karel continued to a small group of disciples who listened intently: "The prince is coming to South Africa to visit South Africans, not a bunch of people he could meet in any old colony!"

Karel's fury inspired outrage in his fellow De Rusters and a lobby was formed. The how-to-get-the-prince-to-stop-at-De Rust lobby and Karel, Gert Meyer, Koos Oosthuizen and Hennie Visser determined to ride four hours to Oudtshoorn in order to discuss the matter with the mayor himself.

The Oudtshoorners were painful, and they did think they were better than the rest, but for all the De Rusters' puff, deep down they felt inferior, and with no briefing, each man in Prinsloo's posse washed his face and put on his church clothes to make the trip to town.

Pressed Pants and Pig Shit

$\mathcal{K}$arel and his men arranged to meet at the station at 5am. Karel, Gert and Koos were punctual. Each man appeared out of the darkness, slightly self-conscious about their attire, which they had never been comfortable wearing even on a Sunday. They pretended not to notice what each other wore. But Hennie did not appear. Then he appeared, all at once, out of a cloud of dust. Galloping. "That stupid bugger is going to tire his horse," scowled Karel and shouted to him to slow. Hennie took no notice, "It's Sol! He's got caught on a fence!" he yelled, "He's going to die if we don't do something." Even in the darkness Hennie's face looked like it had been boiled in lemon juice. He had been crying – hard.

The farmers were accustomed to helping each other without asking too many questions and they followed the panicking friend a mile to his barbed wire boundary and followed the screeching until they made out a gargantuan pig dangling sadly from the wire.

"Shit, what a mess," said Karel. "We will have to get hold of his back legs and tip him over." Hennie was crying, he couldn't help it. He didn't even realise he was until Karel slapped him in the stomach and told him to "come right". Sol was Hennie's best breeding pig. Hennie loved Sol.

Gert and Koos illuminated the scene with their lanterns while Hennie inspected the animal. Now he cried hard, knew it, and didn't care. "His balls are ripped to pieces, we will have to castrate him or he will die!" Generally a reserved man, Hennie had suddenly adopted an almost Shakespearean tone. "But what's the point of that?" said

Karel. "He's a breeding pig. If you castrate him you might as well just kill him now."

"Nooooo!" sobbed Hennie as if Karel had suggested they turn his own mother into bacon.

The ride to Oudtshoorn was a solemn one. Hennie lagged behind so he could cry without annoying anyone, their smart clothing was a mess, but unaccustomed as they were to spruce attire and overt hygiene, the full horror of their appearance didn't strike them as it would others.

"Is the mayor expecting you?" enquired Ina Britz haughtily of the men who stood in her nice clean office reeking of pig shit. "No," grunted Prinsloo, already irritated by her airs. Quite suddenly, Ina, certain that she could not bear the smell as long as it would take to evict the men, pushed open the mayor's door and shooed them inside.

With the door slammed behind them, the stench was sealed in Thys de Beer's plush chamber and the startled mayor paled visibly: "How can I help you gentlemen?" he asked into a large white hand-kerchief bearing his initials in blue, with which he attempted to plug every orifice in his face without suffocating. Karel knew they didn't smell as good as they had done when they had left their homes that morning, but he put the mayor's behaviour down to Oudtshoorn affectation, moved forward and extended his hand. "Karel Prinsloo of De Rust," he said. De Beer reached forward across his desk, afraid to move his feet any closer, and limply shook the enormous paw on offer. Karel began introducing the rest of his party, but de Beer couldn't bring himself to shake any more hands and cut in, saying: "What are you here about Prinsloo?"

"The royal train"

"Oh yes, wonderful news isn't it"

"Well yes and no. We hear that the train is not scheduled to stop at De Rust, only at Oudtshoorn."

"Yes, I believe that's right, otherwise it will be late."

De Beer was pushing the handkerchief so hard into his face now that his words were muffled. "No, now I don't follow," frowned Karel. "What will be great about it? Why will it be great? We don't think there's anything great about it."

"No, no," said de Beer gesturing, "I said otherwise he will be late. Late!"

"Late? Late for what?" asked Karel gravely.

"Late far the ball to be held in his honour. Here in Oudtshoorn."

Karel Prinsloo paused and thought about how best to respond to this fresh, rotten piece of news. Finally, he opted for a philosophical approach. "Perhaps we do not exist," he said more gravely than he had ever said anything in his life and for added drama he leaned across de Beer's polished leather-topped desk as he spoke, bringing him dangerously close to the mayor's nostrils. His question hung in the air like some profound and shaming truth. The posse edged in, dragging their foul auras with them. De Beer struggled not to gag.

"Of course you exist!" exclaimed de Beer, "Of course! But there is nothing I can do about it, because the decision about the prince's journey is the railway's, not mine, you see, not mine. You must go and put your questions to them. Go ask them to stop at your station. I don't care! The station master is Obie Bester, that's who you want, Obie Bester." He scrawled the name on a piece of paper and handed it to Karel.

Ten minutes later a light breeze had refreshed the air in Thys de Beer's office and the posse from De Rust was stinking out the station master's room instead.

Obie Bester was not the mayor, he was not rich and he had not lived under the gentrifying influence of Anne Sutton. "Good God!" he shouted as soon as the lobbyists strode into his small muggy office, "You people smell like shit! Get out! Get out!"

Obie whirled his left arm like a windmill in a hurricane, and pinched the tip of his big, purple nose with the thumb and forefinger of his right.

The five De Rusters, taken aback by the welcome, shuffled along the platform until the station master stopped his herding.

"Why do you stink like that?" begged the immaculate railway-man. "Pigs," answered Karel flatly, "Hennie keeps pigs and we helped castrate one this morning. He was having trouble with it. It got its balls caught on a fence somehow and ripped them badly, so we helped him fix it. We have come to see you about the prince. We're from De Rust."

Obie Bester kept pinching his nose with his right hand and rested the left limply on his hip, affecting a pose suffused with exhaustion. He held the position as though made of wax and listened wearily to Karel's explanation.

When Karel had finished, Obie shifted his gleaming brogues slightly and straightened his gait, then slumped back into the precise pose of before. His mouth hung open, gasping for the air temporari-ly prevented from reaching his lungs through his nostrils. "What the bloody hell are you talking about?" he quacked. "Pigs," began Karel again.

"Stop! I don't mean about the stinking pigs, I mean about the prince. The prince? What about the prince?"

The small, grumpy railway employee, with slicked back hair, great bushy eyebrows, a whispy moustache, and a nose like a dahlia of del-icate mauve, had sucked the wind out of the De Rust contingent's sails and Karel proceeded to state their concerns more politely to Obie Bester than he had done to Thys de Beer. Bester stood, immo-bile, hand on hip, fingers at nose, listening with an impatient heart pumping furiously inside patient posture. Then he took two steps back, released the grip on his nose a moment and coldly announced: "The royal train will make no stop at De Rust," then marched away from the bewildered listeners, fastidiously tugging at his starched white cuffs as he went.

The Driver

South African Railways was an Afrikaans institution. Poor white immigrants, and even cheaper black labour, laid the tracks, but ticket clipping, engine driving and decision making were all the realm of Afrikaners. Given this, Ben Isaac's position was no small feat. In fact, Ben was the most senior driver on the George/Oudtshoorn/Port Elizabeth line. But his appointment came about only because of a tragedy.

The senior driver had been an Afrikaner named Dawie Marais. Whilst holidaying in East London with his wife and six children, Dawie Marais had taken it upon himself to impress two young ladies who had set up brolly and blanket on the sand close by. The brats were off down the beach, four younger boys tormenting two older girls with crabs and seaweed.

"Jean," said the father to his spouse, unusually bright and louder than was necessary, "Did you know that I once saved a life?" Jean, who was watching her children and thinking how she may one day be forced to do just the opposite if they failed to modify their behaviour, did not know that her husband had saved a life. Not just because she had never been told about it, but because Dawie himself had thought up the heroic scenario only a moment before. "Yes, where do you think shoulders like this come from?" he continued, flexing his fairly baggy biceps and furtively glancing at the pretty girls all the time to be sure he had their attention before continuing. The girls giggled at the comedy and were clearly engaged.

"Yes, it was a terrible day. Winter in Port Elizabeth is no joke. There was a howling gale and hardly a person on the beach. I was walking home along the sand, it must have been about fifteen years ago now, I was about nineteen at the time."

Jean began to count back from her husband's forty-five years. while Dawie bulldozed on: "I was still boxing then. I had quite a body I can tell you. Nobody messed with me."

Jean, who had been watching the storyteller in amazement, glanced at the girls, then at the children rushing about in the waves, squealing and carrying some sleeping sunbather's small brown dog off into the foam. Dawie continued. "Then I heard this calling, "Help! Help!" and I look out to sea and there's this head bobbing about out there in the breakers. Quick as anything, I pull off my shoes and jacket and run into the water. It was freezing. I tell you, it gives me goose bumps just thinking about it." He rubbed his arms. "But I didn't care, I knew I had to do something and I just kept swimming."

Dawie paused a moment to enjoy the fascinated looks on the girls' faces a moment. Jean shocked him out of his trance with an impatient, "Well, did you save him?"

"It was a struggle I can tell you, but I managed somehow. But it wasn't a him, it was a her. A young lady. Barely a woman. She was beautiful, very beautiful. She fell in love with me actually."

"Well, where is she now then?" came Jean sarcastically.

"No, I told her not to be so silly. She was only fifteen. I just made sure that she got home to her parents safely and all that."

Then, Hercules, carried away by his own drama, leapt up before his wife could quiz him any further, and jogged down to the shore. He swam out and out, looking back periodically, waving with confidence, then out and out some more. Jean soon tired of the show-off and closed her eyes. It was three minutes before she looked out again, but Dawie was gone.

The body never was found. And so it was that Ben being the only other man who had passed the driver's exam in Port Elizabeth at the time, became the drowned man's replacement. For South African Railways, the tragedy of having to make a Jew the driver to christen the new line far outweighed the one which had left Jean Marais a widow.

Jew

$\mathcal{B}$en's colleagues knew he was a Jew, but they seemed to forgive him for it, and he was allowed to go about his business reasonably un-harassed. He laughed nervously at the Jew jokes they told, did his job well, greeted everyone by their first name and was oddly at ease among them.

Because the Oudtshoorn line was his, Ben comfortably assumed that he would be the one to drive the royal train. He put aside his best overalls as soon as he heard the news, and wore only his other pair to be sure that when the great day came, he would be as neat as a pin.

His beloved wife Hannah, starched and pressed the blue cotton dungarees until they could stand by themselves, and occasionally, when the princely task was being discussed Ben would get so excited he would dress rehearse. Hannah would help him into his outfit - large white kerchief around his short thick neck, blue cap perched at an angle on flocculent head, navy blue dungarees rigidly encasing the soft white body. Then she'd sit and watch as her man strode stiffly around the living room, as if in clothes of cardboard, smiling and tipping his hat and secretly imagining their tiny daughter had survived tuberculosis and could see him now.

Ben was never dejected. Sometimes he came home tired, sometimes mildly irritable, but never depressed. But that fateful Friday evening, as the couple lit their candles and cemented their Sabbath in ancient prayer, Hannah knew something was wrong. Ben refused to speak about it. "It is Shabbat you know," he snapped when she enquired for the third time in half an hour as to what it was that irked him, "Let us eat and pray and not gossip, alright?"

It was Sunday evening before Ben could bring himself to tell Hannah what the matter was. In a further attempt to cheer her husband, Hannah had asked, quite innocently, about the royal train journey. Ben stared past her at first, then tears welled in his eyes: "I knew they never liked me, but I thought they respected me. You know." The next pause was the hardest to break, but finally he sighed and said it. "Hannah, I am not picked to drive the prince's train. Jans Jonker is the one. I'm sorry." He took a short, sharp breath, exhaled deeply. In again, out again, and somehow forced most of his tears back into the pink, fleshy pouches that were his cheeks.

Persuasion

$\mathcal{B}$en Isaac was not the only one who had assumed that he would drive the royal train, most people along the track supposed the same. It was an assumption that threw the De Rust community into a spin for two reasons: Ben Isaac didn't drink, and Ben Isaac was a Jew. How was he to be persuaded to stop the train at their station? What would entice his desire? What would trigger his sympathy?

After the Oudtshoorn disaster, Karel Prinsloo and his supporters were down but not out. They gathered outside the shop that sold everything, bent their heads, furrowed their brows and puffed tobacco in doleful contemplation of their predicament.

"You know the Jews!" burst out Karel, hoping the rhetorical nature of his question would awake any deep-rooted suspicions about the settlers from Eastern Europe, who wore funny hats and favoured the colour black, regardless of whether anyone had died or not. It was a prejudice none present, including himself, had ever felt acutely, after all there were no Jews in De Rust to threaten them, and Ben Isaac was meek enough. But now, with the royal stop at stake, things were different.

After a heavy pause, Karel continued. "Now if the driver was one of us, an Afrikaner, well we might have a chance. But no! The Jew will drive the train, just like everything else. " The precise meaning of this last blame was blurry, but it succeeded in provoking further loathing for the Jew. The Jew who was going to ruin De Rust's chances of a royal visit.

Heads dropped further still and thick, ponderous blasts of smoke engulfed the cabal. The screen door of the shop that sold everything creaked open, then clattered closed and Karel's wife Rosa stood unsuited amongst the men. The serious lot stared at the aproned woman, somewhat bewildered. "What Rosa?" asked Karel irritated, "Can't you see we're thinking?" Rosa grinned inwardly, silently mocking the arrogance of men. "Oh nothing, just some news about the royal train that's all," she said and started back inside. Her husband called her back in a tone which sounded more anxious than he would have liked.

When Rosa made the announcement about Jans Jonker and his grand assignment, the men's stares moved from the shopkeeper's wife, to the shopkeeper's husband, to each other, and finally upwards. Praise the Lord! "Hettie Botha told me yesterday. Jans Jonker is her cousin," Rosa finished, then returned to the shop.

An Afrikaner with close family ties in De Rust to drive the royal train. Each man lost himself in a sapphire, diamond, ruby encrusted fantasy for a moment.

With renewed hope in De Rust of a royal drive by, the five man posse swelled to ten men and a wife, and they set off on their mission the following morning. When the party reached the Botha farm, dear old Hettie was preparing a lunch of onions, pork and porridge for herself and her grandson. The squat woman with black and white hair and small twinkling eyes, rushed outside at the thunderous sound of forty-four approaching hooves, but the sight of all that dust and muscle soon scared her back in. and she bolted the door and flattened herself against one wall and clutched a half-peeled onion to her chest.

Rosa jumped down and called out to her friend, "Hettie, it's me, Rosa Prinsloo. Hettie!" Moments later, the frightened hedgehog unbolted the door, and squinted into the sunlight, wet-faced from onion tears, and smiling.

Hettie's house was unable to accommodate such a large party, so the women made coffee and served the men outside while Karel got right down to business: they'd come about the royal train. Which her cousin was going to drive. Which wasn't scheduled to stop at De Rust. But that they wanted to stop at De Rust. But that the station master had said no to their request. And so Jans Jonker was their only hope.

Hettie didn't understand. "But what has all this got to do with me?"

Her relationship to the driver of course.

"Yes, but I don't work for the railways."

No they knew that, but she could introduce them to her cousin – the driver – who did work for the railways, and was going to drive the prince's train. Perhaps they could persuade him to stop at De Rust.

"But I can't change train schedules."

No, but perhaps her cousin could.

Finally Hettie understood, and a visit to the cousin who lived seven miles south in a village called Bloodyfar, was arranged.

It was Sunday afternoon when cousin Hettie, ten men, and a wife knocked unexpectedly on Jans Jonker's door. The driver was napping off a large lunch and Hettie's tentative tapping did not stir him, and as he had no wife to answer all was still.

It had been a long journey (Bloodyfar, although only seven miles away, got its name because it felt so very much further away from anywhere than that), and when a third attempt by Hettie to rouse the occupant failed, an impatient Karel Prinsloo banged on the wood so hard Jans Jonker yipped into consciousness.

Once he was over the rude awakening, the party was invited to sit wherever they could while Hettie fussed about the place, trying in five minutes to add the woman's touch it had always dodged. Jans didn't like women, and women were hardly queuing to persuade him to change his mind. He was in his early forties and had a belly the size and shape of a large watermelon – only not so firm. Most of the hair on his head sprouted around his chin and ears while on top lived just a few soft sandy wisps, like baby hair. He liked to cook and liked to eat even more, and he enjoyed a glass of brandy in the company of men, but his disposition was prosaic and he had no real friends. He took his job especially seriously and had lost no sleep over snatching the royal task away from the Jew.

Jans had been a mere crossing keeper when the railways lost Dawie Marais, and the calamity of Isaac being left to christen the new line affected him deeply. Within three months the young Afrikaner had studied for and passed the drivers' exam himself to safeguard against any such thing ever happening again. He disliked the Jews. He disliked many people.

Jonker lived in a house not much bigger than those of the farmers who crammed it now. The interior looked startlingly like its occupant: dull, with hair in all the wrong places. (The culprit cat snoozed enormously on the kitchen table throughout the visit.)

To kick things off nicely the driver was ceremoniously presented with a bottle of brandy, made with care in De Rust. Jonker and Prinsloo congratulated one another on their taste in liquor. Then, keen to reassure each other of their decency, they stressed that they only drank the stuff on the rarest of Sundays, but this being a special occasion the bottle was opened and some of its contents poured into just two of the four mugs, which had been hastily rounded up by Hettie.

Karel was a simple man, but he understood the power of flattery and launched into his accolade at once. "Let me say, right off, that we at De Rust think it a fine thing that an Afrikaner, and not a Jew, will drive the royal train. And let me also say, that we at De Rust think that you are the best Afrikaner for the job." The serious fat man clearly enjoyed the Sun King's speech and nodded his head in affirmation of his own qualities.

"We at De Rust would also like to say what a valuable member of our community your cousin is," continued Karel indicating Hettie whose name he hardly ever knew and now forgot entirely. "And, let me say, that we are a community of Afrikaners, like yourself, but that we, like yourself, are great admirers of royalty and, of course, the prince."

In the course of such verbose admiration and lofty ideas, Prinsloo had downed two large shots of brandy in as many gulps and was proved correct in his assumption that their host would follow suit, to show that he was a man worthy of the praise he was soliciting.

"But we have a problem," continued Karel, solemn now, "It is a problem that not even the mayor of Oudtshoorn can solve." Dramatic pause. More brandy poured and swallowed. "In fact, we believe that you are the only man *alive* who can solve it."

Four drinks into the monologue, the speaker in the battered fedora paused deliberately, then looked straight at the man with the baby scalp and said, "We need you to stop the royal train briefly at De Rust."

The silence that ensued was dense with anticipation. Jans Jonker began to fumble with his empty glass, and shook his head. Karel Prinsloo leapt swiftly into the space about to accommodate refusal, "Just for an instant. A couple of minutes. Hardly any time at all! Almost more of a – slowing down." Karel poured as he spoke. This time Jonker didn't need much time to drink up, and a sigh of relief rippled through the audience as he slurped. Then the driver slowly prepared to speak. He stroked his beard to indicate discernment, cleared his throat and heaved out his reply: "I would like to help, of course, but I can't." At this Prinsloo raised his glass and said simply, "Of course. We understand." His disciples gasped in horror. Was this their leader? Where was his fight? But the leader paid them no attention, kept his eyes on Jonker and another tipple was swallowed. As the sixth drink settled into De Rust's last hope, his drunkenness was suddenly apparent. He loosened his tie and giggled briefly to himself, then he recovered and reiterated his limitations. "No I really can't. Sorry." Karel, still comfortably in command of all his faculties, now changed the subject. "Tell me Jonker, are you enjoying our special De Rust brandy?" Jonker's head went up and down. Karel poured him another tot and nudged his wife to fetch more, ten bottles more.

Jans Jonker was a tough nut to crack, but crack he did. Another half litre of the honey-coloured liquid and he agreed to toot three times as the royal train approached De Rust, and slow right down, almost to a standstill as it pulled through the station.

With this promise secure, the jubilant party took their leave, glancing back briefly at the figure of Jans Jonker, swaying in the door-way of his tiny house, batting back the waves they sent him, before he banged down hard on his belly, which, had it in fact been a melon, would have splattered with the force and made a sticky mess all over.

The De Rusters did not look back again and so never noticed the driver fall. They were too busy looking ahead, to the future, to De Rust, where the prince would indeed stop at the platform behind the shop that sold everything. On the way home the party was mostly quiet, dreaming about the event that would crown their lives.

Once Hettie had been gently delivered back to her small swept box like some previously unnoticed premium, it was Hennie's voice that pierced the quiet. "Karel," he said.

"Yes," said Karel.

"Did you think there was anything funny about that Jonker guy?"

"Funny? What do you mean 'funny'?" said Karel more nettled than curious. The counter question was too much for Hennie and he wished he'd said nothing at all. "No, no he's fine. I don't even know what I mean," he said and they carried on dreaming again.

Party

*T*he Saturday evening following Karel Prinsloo's triumph at Bloodyfar, a celebratory dance was held in De Rust. The event took place outside the shop that sold everything, with a huge camp fire illuminating the site. The thrust of the evening's chatter was of course, the royal slowdown.

Karel made a speech early on, before everyone got too drunk to appreciate it. It was an emotional address, rife with confused patriotisms: "Because we are proud to be South Africans – Afrikaners, and we are proud that they are royals, and we are proud of each other, and that the prince will be proud to have been here among us and everything like that." Karel's spirits were at such a zenith that he was even moved to mention the recently castigated Ben Isaac: "It isn't that I don't like the Jew, it's just that we think that this is now a better arrangement – you know!" The mimic made the people roar, and Karel's wit, generosity and ascendancy that Saturday night secured him celebrity status in De Rust for the rest of his life.

The festivities included dancing to the strains of Harry Joubert's drunken accordion, the consumption of twenty six bottles of brandy, and the manifestation of Eban September.

An outsider landing amongst locals was a rarity in itself, but an outsider the colour of jet seemed well nigh impossible, and revellers blinked in disbelief as Eban September entered the throng, bold, arrogant even. He was a wiry man in his mid-twenties with intense black eyes and twisted tendrils of knotted black hair sticking up all over his head. He had purposely shredded his dirty brown trousers into coarse filthy ribbons that swished dramatically as he moved.

He slunk into the throng so gracefully, so quietly, that he had penetrated its heart before he was noticed. The people stopped dancing and the crowd parted like some Biblical ocean as he passed through them. Harry Joubert's instrument farted and hiccoughed to a halt and everyone waited for Karel to see the intruder. When he did he stared incredulous a moment, then drew enough breath to spit his enquiry. But before he could release the words, the pitch intruder looked straight at him and in a deep, velvety voice said, "I 'ant ot dnce."

No-one stirred. Even Karel Prinsloo was momentarily lost for words. How dare this black devil interrupt their festival with his drivel?

"Can yo hear ear em? I 'ant ot dnce."

Now Karel found his voice: "I don' t know what the hell you're saying! Get out! Get away before I whip you!"

Karel turned his back to indicate that the thing was finished. Then suddenly too curious, he twisted round to look at the devil again. But it was too late, it had already trotted back through the people and receded into the darkness from whence it came.

The crowd muttered and Harry Joubert's accordion belched, spluttered and wheezed into a waltz.

Friendship

Eban September was not an hallucination, he was a traveller and an artist who made shapes and signs with his lithe, supple body. Sometimes his dance would earn him a few coins. More often he had to steal his supper.

When Eban arrived at De Rust on his way from nowhere to who-can-say-where, he encountered Thomas Eland.

Always courteous, Thomas tipped his hat at the curious figure loping through the veld towards him like a panther in casual search of prey. The raggedy man stopped abruptly and looked at the thin, graceful leathery one who greeted him. Eban stretched out both hands, palms up, and without shifting his deadpan expression said, "Mi brthor. I will ste thiw uoy."

Thomas Eland, good soul that he was, understood exactly what the stranger had said and didn't think it odd. He thought that the way the stranger had said it was merely a sign from God, who, in his infinite wisdom, had sent this bizarre spirit to be near him.

The traveller and his new friend hardly spoke a word more as they made their way to Eland's home.

That sunset Mary Eland was fiercely religious. The same filthy yellow dress, so often unbuttoned to her midriff and hiked up to her waist, was fastened awkwardly to the neck and hung down to her ankles. The unruly hair was kept in check by a green cotton scarf that Ruth had given her. She wore her only pair of shoes, lace-ups that used to belong to Abel Lategan. The leather was hard and cracked and there was four sizes too much of it, which made her shuffle rather than walk for fear that she might fall out of them otherwise.

"God bless you Eban September. God bless you." She kept repeating and hugged the stranger more times that evening than he had been hugged the whole of his life. Each touch sent a shock through his body that made him stiff as wood and stopped him breathing a moment. The alien embrace frightened, baffled and seduced him all at once.

That night Mary, fairly demented with faith, tackled the role of dutiful Christian wife with a vigour that exhausted her audience.

"Give me your hand. Give," Mary ordered and clutched at Eban and Thomas' hands as heartily as if they were preparing to support the balancing act of a two hundred pound acrobat, then closing her eyes and lifting her chin towards God, she was off: "Oh Lord Jesus! Please make a blessing here on all of us! Please! Please come into our lives and make us good like you – like you want us to be. We are sinners! We sin so terrible! And we know we will be punished! And now please dear Jesus make a blessing on our food and – thank you Jesus for all the things you give us, and that you give us Eban September we thank you, oh Lord our saviour ... and ... and ..." The praying lasted several minutes before it reached *Amen*, and when Eban opened his eyes after a moment's pause he jumped slightly at the sight of Mary's peg-toothed grin, which she had brought up close while he had still been blind. Thomas smiled, sadly, proudly, and touched Mary's arm in a gesture of thanks.

Mary hardly ate. Her biblical quizzing took her mouth away from her food. Her parables were as muddled as her hair but Eban September listened politely and nodded at what she said which was enough to have Mary believe he might love her. In truth he had never shared a meal with a woman so deranged and was repulsed. When Thomas suggested an early night Eban leapt from the table enthusiastically and curled up near the hearth, eyes closed, and the tiring charade was stopped until morning.

From the moment Eban September arrived in the Eland

household, something happened to Mary. Her thirst for liquor was replaced by a hunger for Eban's approval. It was his aloofness rather than any overt display of religiousness that somehow convinced her that piety would be the best way to win his love. She was so infatuated that she never dreamed of anything so low as brazen sexual innuendo as a means of conquering the fleshy pink heart that throbbed within the hard, smooth ebony shell. She would give up the drink.

Mary shivered, shat and vomited. She cowered as flocks of flying ostrich swooped inches above her head. She itched and tingled convinced a million lice were burrowing beneath her skin, but she would not touch the stuff that could banish the plague. She lay low while her body expelled the demons. She stayed in the bedroom with the door closed and made sure that only Thomas witnessed the horror.

"Please don't tell Eban. Please don't tell him," she pleaded.

Her husband held her hand and trickled soup into her and promised that her recovery would be the secret of just the three of them: himself, herself and their Lord.

When Mary emerged two weeks later, the bond between Thomas and Eban was already complete. The dancer accompanied his friend on all his chores. He baled lucerne and fed chickens and carried drums of water that hurt the older man to lift. Thomas marvelled at his friend's physical strength and spiritual fearlessness. Eban admired his friend's faith, kindness and patience.

The glorious umber dusk when Thomas Eland returned home to find a clean, pretty, sober wife, he could not stop his tears. He cried so much he could not speak, and when Mary and Eban tried to comfort him, he covered his face. He staggered outside, fell to his knees and whispered prayers of thanks throughout the night.

Angel

Ten years Ruth and Hannes stayed at Vlakteplaas. One hundred and twenty months of Van der Want's rule they endured. The decision to settle there had been made for rather than by them. They had run out of food and had been unsuccessful in securing work elsewhere. Yes, they could work for Van der Want, but no, they would never earn enough to leave. They would hardly earn enough to survive, and they would take not a moment's pleasure in any of it. But death in the dust was their only alternative, so they took the employment. Besides, they had a daughter to consider.

After leaving De Rust, Ruth and Hannes trudged through the vastness hardly meeting a soul, moving from one farm to the next. They talked nothing of infidelity or drunkenness, just moved together, sad, gentle, quiet, anticipating the possibility of starvation or attack with the resignation granted to those who live in hell but believe in heaven.

By day they were adrift in an ocean of heat waves, by night they lost themselves in one galaxy after another, enjoying the cool relief the stars brought with them and the discreet comfort of lying close.

At dawn on the third day they were woken by a sound so alien that they did not recognise it at first as human. The soft sobbing seemed to come from every direction and none at all. The couple propped themselves on their elbows and tilted their heads trying to locate the distress. Suddenly the sound spoke and the strangeness of the moment was complete. "Here," said a child's voice, right behind them.

Ruth called her Angel. The child had no other name she would admit to, so it stuck.

Hannes had been married briefly when he was nineteen, but before their first anniversary, his wife had died as she gave birth to a child that flopped from her womb limp and blue and silent.

Ruth had failed to fall pregnant during the time she had been with Hannes and she mourned the fact. But now their merciful Lord had sent them an Angel. The girl looked about five years old. Either abandoned or lost, she wore a torn blue dress and had no name. She seemed fearless around the couple, and they concluded that she had perhaps not been abused so much as neglected and then finally abandoned, possibly more out of poverty than heartlessness.

Angel would not answer most of their questions: Where was her Mammie? Where was her Pappie? Was she lost? Where did she come from? Was she hungry? "Ja!" The answer gripped Ruth and Hannes with a new sense of urgency, and in an instant, giving up and dying there in wilderness was erased from their minds as a possibility. They reached Vlakteplaas later that day, went round to Van der Want's back door with one of his labourers, and so entered into slavery.

Angel was beautiful. She was not white and she was not black and she was not even brown like Hannes and Ruth. Her hair was like coils of tarnished copper wire, and although her skin was darkish, her eyes were green, like Ruth's. She spoke Afrikaans well. She even recognised the Bible when Ruth showed it to her.

"I know Jesus. He lives in that book," she said.

"But who told you this Angel?" Ruth would entreat, unable to believe that such a child had no name, no family, no love. But Angel would always say she just knew, and then avoid more questions, usually by posing some of her own about a bird or the clouds.

Hannes had become withdrawn since his shameful demise, but now he forgot all that whenever he looked at the foundling. He enjoyed his turns to keep her with him while he worked. He'd teach her little songs, how to count her fingers, toes, feathers, eggs, stones.

He made up stories to amuse her. He'd let her tickle his ribs while he begged for mercy. Hannes believed that Angel was what God had intended for the world. She would never be a Mary Wynand. She would never be a Hannes Willemse. She would be an Eland, never tempted by lust or liquor. Tears often welled in his eyes when he looked at her, "Angel," he'd say, "you are what God meant when he made the world, do you know that?" She would stare uncomprehending, then carry on with whatever she had set herself to do to help with that day's horrendous load. The first couple of years at Vlakteplaas, Ruth and Hannes lived in fear of the child's parents coming to take her away, perhaps even charging them with kidnapping. But no one ever did come, and the more time that passed, the less the possibility distressed them. It was ten years before she was snatched, but by nobody like a parent.

Van der Want had seen the unusual child the day the Elands arrived looking for work. He had noted her beauty lasciviously even though she was an infant. He rarely saw her after that, but whenever he did he mused with satisfaction on her good looks which grew along with her limbs, and he let his mind linger on unspeakable perversions.

Ten years after the first sighting, as Van der Want rode through his lands, he noticed the head of copper glinting in the sun. It was a beacon in a field of emerald lucerne. She was alone. He rode slowly over to her. Angel pretended at first not to notice and continued her harvesting without looking up. But Van der Want moved his horse so close that she was finally forced to stand upright and look to avoid being trampled.

She had never spoken a word to the master before. Now she did so politely "Morning," she said then stared down again at the lush green crop. Van der Want said nothing, just ran his eyes all over her. She was not very tall, but she had well-developed breasts and a face that could not have suited her name better. He wanted to see her legs.

"Lift up your skirt," he said.

Since Isadora Bloomfield, and besides his wife, Van der Want had not had sex with another white woman. Instead he paid a pittance to the drunken parents of young coloured girls in exchange for rape. But Angel was different. She was not very white but she was not quite coloured. No money was paid, no parent or husband consulted, lust was the only consideration as he plundered the virgin so viciously and so repeatedly it almost killed her.

Angel's screams were terrible but nobody came. Erma heard her all the way from the house, but helplessness had long ago over-whelmed compassion. Now she just stood on the verandah, trying to listen for birdsong and thought about the bread she had baking. Some of the poor white tenants and coloured labourers heard and stopped what they were doing, chilled despite the scorching day, by the sounds Angel made. They were fairly sure of what the horror was and just shook their heads and continued silently with their work, ashamed. Ruth and Hannes were together that day at the mill and heard nothing over the grinding of stone on corn.

After a while Angel stopped her wailing, not because the pain was gone, and not because it brought no help but because her attacker seemed to enjoy it. Her cries confirmed his power over the area. Nobody came and nobody would dare try to stop him even if they had been standing right there watching. He almost wished they were.

That evening, Ruth and Hannes found Angel curled up and whim-pering on her mattress. When the one thing that God had meant when he created the world finally did manage to whisper the nature of her vio-lation there was a sound like the snap of brittle steel as Hannes' heart broke. Despite her own agony, Ruth was forced into the role of com-forter once more. After that Hannes would not speak. Sometimes he broke things or slammed his body into walls, and there were moments when it seemed as if the strange groaning sounds he made might sud-denly form words, but the helplessness of knowing that he would be shot before he came within twenty yards of Duppie du Plessis' six fancy steps in search of revenge kept him in pain and incoherent.

Roller-skates

The invention of the wheel had certainly been useful to the good people of Oudtshoorn but it had never been so much fun. Four tiny ones, roughly two inches in diameter, secured to the sole of each foot, ensured hours of enjoyment for folk of all ages, and if one managed to glide and pirouette with grace, it even increased one's chances of acceptance into the bosom of Oudtshoorn society.

Roller-skates were introduced to feather heaven by Lady Agatha Teeling-Smith. The instant a drawing of this modern recreational tool first leapt out at her from the sepia pages of an issue of *Critchley's Bazaar*, she knew she had to have a pair.

Agatha's standing in Oudtshoorn as an icon of style was due in no small part to her long-standing subscription to that high fashion society magazine, *Critchley's*. Others soon cottoned onto this source of much chic and also subscribed, but a simple transaction between the first reader and the postmaster ensured that everyone else received their copy some days later than herself, which gave her just the head start she needed to mention, order, or make the latest thing from England before anybody else did.

To the late recipients of this bible, it was as perplexing as it was infuriating, but whenever the postmaster George Hocking was questioned on the matter, he would scratch his cheek and say how he couldn't think how such a thing could happen. He would then further enrage enquirers by casting a crude net of doubt over the truth of their claims.

"Are you sure you get yours later than Lady Agatha gets hers?"

he'd ask innocently. And philosophically he'd suggest, "I'm sure, if that is the case, then she must sometimes get hers later than you get yours."

Agatha paid George Hocking the enormous sum of three pounds per annum for the service, so he did not mind searching earnestly through sacks and pigeonholes in an attempt to unravel the mystery for any outraged who demanded that he did. But alas, for all his searching he never did manage to crack the conundrum.

Agatha's roller skate discovery ranked among her most vogueish and was certainly her most popular. Conveniently enough there had been a coupon to snip from the bottom of the advertisement and she cut round it, attached a postal order to it, sent it off, and waited excitedly for a pair to arrive, which they did, eventually, by post. She relished her conviction that no other socialite in town would have the imagination to do the same even once they did dissect their *Critchley's* September issue, and she was right.

The skates arrived six weeks later. Nessie Plaatjies laced the things onto madam's boots, laughing all the time: "Oo Madam this is the funniest things in the world. Like two little donkey carts for you to stand on. Maybe you should get two little donkeys to pull you along."

A full six weeks Agatha practiced. She hobbled and slipped across her smooth kitchen floorboards, grabbing for balance wherever she could and sending pots crashing into walls, doors slamming into frames and utensils pinging to the floor as she went.

Nessie squealed with a mixture of fright and joy as her madam came flying towards her. "You going to kill yourself!" she'd wail, catching the large regal figure, which was so unbelievably hunched and flailing. One morning, after a couple of highly successful laps of the kitchen, an especially confident madam took an unexpected turn and hurtled down the long, narrow passageway towards her servant. It felt good at first: "I'm coming Nessie! Look at me! I'm magnificent!" she hollered, then rammed straight into a saucer-eyed Nessie Plaatjies who was kneeling to polish the front door's brass at the time.

After the crash the petite brown woman lay crushed beneath the substantial white one, neither able to shift for some time, more for their laughter than their pain.

The upshot of the tumble was a small swelling on the back of Nessie's head and a diet for madam. "My dear it's shocking!" declared Agatha, appalled at herself, "I could have *killed* you. My great bulk, plonking down on top of you like that. I *insist* you starve me."

Her passion for roller-skating outlived the diet and at the end of the training, Agatha emerged, no smaller, but splendid on eight wheels.

Their first day out on skates, Nessie wore her finest to escort her madam. The battered blue hat, which had once rested elegantly on madam's head, drooped on hers, badly misshapen as it was after an unfortunate encounter with a curious bird. On her feet she wore a pair of navy blue leather boots, recently re-heeled for the third time. Around the top of her left arm, beneath her dress, she had pinned a thick woolen sock, intended as padding against madam's grip, which she knew could be fierce depending on her state of balance.

In stockinged feet, Agatha towered a full five inches over her maid. In skates the difference grew to eight. Had Nessie taken this into account she might have thought it as well to tie a sock around her neck. The skater was no more or less grandly clad than usual. A dozen strings of pearls rested boldly on her enormous bosom, and two huge black plumes in her hat fluttered beautifully in the breeze as she went. Their route had been meticulously worked out beforehand. Agatha's house was conveniently situated close to all the most important ports of call: the bank, the post office, Hatfield's Department Store, The Queen's Hotel. But success was disconcertingly slow. The bank was unusually quiet for a Thursday, and the only person who stared at the skates was a common sort of woman in a gimcrack hat who boldly asked – in Afrikaans no less – "What you got on your feet?"

"Roller skates of course," snapped Agatha in reply with as much indignation as if questioned about the colour of her underwear. Then she left, as gracefully as she could, exerting enough pressure on Nessie Plaatjies's arm to have drawn blood, were it not for the sock. Things weren't much better at the post office. George Hocking was suitably enchanted: "Must be another *Critchley's Bazaar* thing," he said. "It's a miracle of the modern world, those shoes Lady Agatha. A miracle." But his reaction was hardly of any importance. It wasn't until they reached Hatfield's Department Store that the dedicated practice finally paid off. Agatha kept score of the number of smart ladies she encountered and Nessie was instructed to keep count too. Three at the perfume counter, four in millinery, one trying on shoes, two at the sweet counter, two in haberdashery and five buying gloves.

"How many Nessie?"

"Sixteen. "

"Are we counting Mrs Brimes?"

"Ja."

"Good."

Tea at the Queen's Hotel and the number of suitably astonished swelled to nineteen, and by the time Nessie was rubbing madam's feet in the comfort of the Teeling-Smith drawing room, the two were drunk with success.

Preparations: De Rust

The shop that sold everything had never sold so much of it. Special orders were placed for more than the everything it already shelved. Fabric was most popular. Fabric, lace, ribbon, everything pretty enough for a royal visit/stop/slowdown.

The brown people who expressed an interest in the prince were actively discouraged from getting too excited. This was white people's business, and, "The prince was not to be subjected to a bunch of drunken Hottentots at De Rust!" said the whites. But the brown people sewed themselves new outfits from old curtains, and discussed the regal coming just the same.

Karel's standing in the community soared throughout the preparations. He elevated himself to the position of host and his followers and neighbours were mostly glad to kowtow to his suggestions about how things should be arranged. His instructions were given during formal meetings in the church where Karel would instruct from the pulpit: "Children will stand in front, although there will of course have to be men stationed at intervals along the edge of the platform to make sure that nobody gets hurt. The committee has also agreed that it would be too formal for the men to take their hats off when the train passes." Karel did have his detractors and a handful of them muttered half-heartedly as he spoke and fixed their eyes on the battered green felt agglutination on his head and wished it would move down over the face, wrap around the neck and throttle the speaker. Who made him the boss of everything in De Rust anyway? However, he was the popular choice.

"We think that waving would be the most natural thing to do, but no shouting out. We don't want the prince to think we're a bunch of savages." The rest of the meeting was spent discussing the problem of the brown people, an issue that had recently become highlighted.

Four days earlier, as Karel dismounted his horse outside the shop that sold everything, the black devil who had disrupted their Jans Jonker celebrations appeared again, seemingly from nowhere. Prinsloo started slightly then recovered, but a feeling of dread and fury began to scorch at his centre. Eban stood still and watched the boss man undo the girth of his saddle and pretend not to notice him. But seconds later, the big red man could stand the black's impudent look no longer. "What?! What do you want you bugger?!" he cried. Eban said nothing, just began to move his body into extraordinary signs and shapes, all the time staring straight at Karel. The shop-keeper had never seen anything like it before. It was as compelling as it was unsettling and to conceal his wonderment he began to laugh. He called to the traders under the poplar trees to come and join in his amusement. It didn't take long for the gathering to get carried away, mimicking, jeering, and even throwing small stones at the sight.

Rosa and two shoppers rushed out to see what the noise was about. Eban continued, as if in a trance, keeping up an impossibly slow perpetual motion, unfolding one long supple leg up past his ear while the other bent and stretched beneath him. His arms made waves and angles that told a story of something familiar yet abstract. His face remained set as stone. Each giggler knew somehow that their foolish twittering was all that kept them from being bewitched by the dance and so their laughter grew. Then Eban September's voice sliced unexpectedly through the mocking sounds. He stood still and spoke loudly: "I 'ont ot d'nce for th' prinz."

Now the watchers roared all the more. They laughed too hard to speak. They clutched one another and someone imitated the stranger's speech. Then Rosa Prinsloo stepped forward. Her hand-some face was contorted into a look that neither her husband nor anyone else present had ever seen before. "What's so funny? Hey?" she said. "This man is an artist. What's so funny about that?" Karel froze. His Rosa had never spoken any differently about the kaffirs than anybody else. She was never cruel or harsh, but she had never stood up for them either. Not that he could remember. Not even the time Hennie tied a supposed thief to his saddle and dragged him around the village at a canter for fifteen minutes. Not even the time Deon Meiring denied his workers an hour off to go to a funeral. But now she was upset! And not even over one of her workers, but over a strange black devil from nowhere at all!

"That's enough Rosa. Get back in the shop!" roared Karel. Rosa stayed a moment then started back towards the store. Eban September was shooed away and the crowd dispersed awkwardly.

Fear consumed Karel Prinsloo. He had never seen his wife so angry, so passionate about anything. It bothered him. Rosa was no lamb, she had opinions of her own and occasionally even expressed them, but nothing like this. This outburst. And over a black man. A black devil.

Unable to face her right away. Karel pulled the girth tight around his horse again and rode off, away from Rosa, to think a while.

The more he thought about it, the more his mind filled with images of his wife making love to Eban September. That night, still unable to think of any reason other than lust for Rosa's behaviour, with one blow, Karel broke Rosa's jaw. It was the only thing he could think of to say.

Word of the saga spread quickly. Even Thomas Eland heard and told his friend. Eban was anxious "I 'ill see if esh's a–right." Thomas implored him not to. "It's a white man's wife Eban. Leave it," he said.

But his friend raised his hand to indicate that he had heard and walked away, towards De Rust. When Thomas returned home that evening without Eban, Mary became hysterical. "They'll kill him!" Then she asked more quietly, "Does he love her?" Thomas did his best to calm his wife, "They won't kill him. No, he doesn't love her."

But it was useless, she just cried and screamed and lashed out at Thomas when he tried to settle her. Around midnight Eban September returned, unscathed. He was bewildered by the fuss the pair made over him and only said that the lady was okay, then lay down on his mattress and slept.

"The coloureds seem to think they can become involved some-how," continued Karel, "but the committee is clear on this, they must be kept away at all costs. So we have come up with a plan, but I think Dominee Wessels should explain. Dominee."

The man of God, who was as small on the inside as he was on the outside, plodded up the podium as though it were the last five steps of some great summit. On arriving at the top, he lifted his head tri-umphantly, and began. "We all know the coloured people. Some of them try to be good, but we know that they are not like us. Their ways are not naturally the ways of Christian people. Christianity is a natu-ral state of being for us whites, it is not like that with them, but I think we all know that." Here he squeezed his small flat red face into a smile that had no teeth and no eyes, before continuing. "And the prince also knows that, I am sure. So it is our duty to guide the coloureds on the day of the royal visit just the way we need to guide them every day. Because if we do not then it will be worse for them, worse for us, and worse for the prince." Another grimace to the crowd. "So we will organise a wonderful treat for them, because they have unfortunately heard about the prince already. I heard some coloureds who work on Sampat le Roux's farm going what-and-what about the King and Queen, and soup, and gold, and I don't know what all, the other day outside Karel's shop. So because they know we must make something nice for them that day. We tell them it's a pic-nic in celebration of the coming of the prince and that it is especially for them. Which of course it is. But it will be the other side of Meiringspoort by the river so they will be out of the way of the track for sure."

The spiritually enlightened continued with many details: the church would provide all the refreshments and even help with transporting them there. The ladies of the church committee would organise food and all the good people at the meeting were asked to contribute in whatever way they could.

The man of God droned on as always, dragging out every point as if each word he uttered was somehow precious simply because it had emanated from his lips. The crowd clapped each time he paused in the hopes that it might bring the monologue to a swifter end, but the Dominee took the first five rounds of appreciation as encouragement, and was only finished at the sixth.

The speech proved as popular as it was tedious and hands shot up all over the room volunteering assistance for the man's inspired scheme. "It will be a nice day for the coloureds," he concluded, "and it will also stop them getting drunk and getting themselves run down by the royal train, which would be very embarrassing."

After the meeting many of the De Rusters wondered to each other how one man could be so clever. How one man could be so virtuous.

Preparations: Oudtshoorn

Preparations in Oudtshoorn were on a much grander scale than those of De Rust. The coloured people there were not even a consideration, so robust were their plans.

Tidy white citizens would gather at the station where a gangway would rope off a wide enough gap to allow the prince and his entourage a comfortable passage through an arc of bunting and out to waiting carriages. Three hundred yards of red carpet had already arrived from England, and it was agreed between all the warring parties that the scarlet path should ultimately lead up the steps of the Queen's Hotel and into the grand hall, where a glittering ball would be held in His Highness's honour.

With wealth in Oudtshoorn came the ability to travel, and with this came a miscellany of frivolous European pastimes: pierrot troupes (at one time, five in total), a thriving ballet school providing graceful entertainment at many fancy functions, cycling elevated to a virtual art form with teams of acrobatic riders competing bi-annually for victory in skill and apparel, among others.

Such fun merrily occupied wealthy farmers, too sophisticated now to occupy themselves with anything more constructive. Costumes were a vital part of all these dramatic pursuits. Ballet nymphs, who generally managed not much more than toe pointing, vague leg lifting and tiny hops into the air, were draped in layers of costly organza. Fey pierrots drooped about in the best French satin. And cyclists were often stuffed into costumes so elaborate they found it impossible to perform some of their trickier stunts. But the advent of Agatha

Teeling-Smith's roller-skates changed how socialising was done in the region considerably. Everyone who was anyone had a pair. The status they ensured meant people shopped in them, dined in them, danced in them, and those with talents such as singing or playing the harp were suddenly forced to wear skates whilst doing so if they were to receive the desired acclaim.

There were some who loathed the fad. Everyone ordered skates and practiced in secret, threatening servants with dismissal or worse if they told a soul about the bumps and falls. But some never did conquer the sport, and they hurled the beastly foot gear into the attic and thereafter huffed whenever they encountered a skater. Others like Thys and Sara de Beer, were fairly hopeless but believed they had a talent for it.

It was Sara who drove the skating process and kept spirits up. Thys, who had rejected the "stupid bloody things" the morning his had arrived, amiably allowed the stupid bloody things to be strapped to his feet the following night after enjoying a particularly pleasurable evening of brandy and pampering at Rosie Botha's.

Anne Sutton stood by and peered disapprovingly as Sara tried to force her husband's colossal brogues onto the metallic movers. The main problem was that Sara, eager to get going, had had her own skates on since morning and flailed at the task considerably.

"I'll take no part in it," declared Anne Sutton as it became clear that help of a physical nature was needed, and she called her servant Lulu van Tonder to leave the dishwashing and assist.

Lulu, a woman of kindly disposition and enormous hips, with not one spot upon her entire being susceptible to the prodding of humour, fell upon the task with as much confidence as she might have in the sweeping of a hearth. Sara de Beer fiddled with the length of one skate while Lulu took the other and clamped it heartily to her master's shoe. Lulu's bustling soon became the new focus of the cackling de Beers' mirth: "Lulu you're a wonder," said Thys, "You attack the problem like it was a ostrich with its arse stuck in a drain or something. Pulling and pushing." Lulu said nothing and just yanked the ends of Thys de Beer's legs about until the skates were on, and made to leave. "No, Lulu, you must help me with the boss," said Sara, staggering to her skates using her husband's head as if it were a banister.

With a woman on either side, one unsteady on eight wheels, the other firm and almost as large as the Rock of Gibraltar, Thys de Beer was hauled upright like the side of a barn. But only for a second before the rollers propelled his lower legs forward without warning, causing him to crash back onto the Chinese silk upholstery like a felled oak. For almost an hour the De Beers toppled about the room laughing and complaining and whooping and puffing.

In time Sara de Beer became reasonably steady on skates. Her husband never did learn to glide, but he enjoyed the challenge and thought the way he lifted one bent leg at a time then crashed it down two inches in front of him like some lumbering marionette was rather fun and he believed it to be, simply, his own unique skating style.

When Agatha proposed that proof of Oudtshoorn's up-to-the-minute tastes would best be displayed to the royal guest by holding a roller-skate, fancy-dress ball, the idea – too avant-garde for anyone in Oudtshoorn to recognise it as such, was passed by an overwhelmingly positive majority.

The night the decision was made, the non-skaters wept into their pillows. The defeated were so pathetic that even Agatha pitied them and at the next Royal Committee meeting she made a noble speech about solidarity and respect and togetherness, and by the end of it the winners were sufficiently moved to such magnanimity that it was agreed that the ball would begin in shoes and that the donning of skates would be optional later on. The losers, having assumed that they would have to miss the event entirely due to their deficiency, were pleased with the compromise and for about a fortnight Oudtshoorn's smart set was seized with a sense of goodwill towards one another the likes of which Christmas alone rivalled.

The Infant of Prague

Royalty had been an important part of Eban September's life since childhood and much of his imagination had developed around the idea.

When he was three months old, his mother took herself and the child to a convent. Four days the coloured woman walked with her too-dark baby strapped to her back before she reached the red-roofed, curved-walled, whitewashed Sacred Heart sanctuary. The building stood strange and lonely among the great lush Outeniqua mountains and her arrival was greeted with some surprise. How did she ever find them? She wouldn't say, just begged to spend the night and said that she was on her way to visit family in George. The nuns couldn't turn her away, so they fed her bread and soup and showed her into a cell, empty but for a bed, a blanket, and a crucifix.

When everyone was asleep, Eban's mother ran away. She took the blanket with her and left the sleeping bundle of boy behind.

The nuns cared for the child as they might have done a dog, with stern kindness and bland nourishment, fleeting affection and little else. They drummed their religious beliefs into him as a matter of course and Eban lapped up every word. He loved this tremendous God who hung in the sky and saw everything that everybody did, and could even read our thoughts. He loved the serene statues of Mother Mary that greeted him with open palms around each corner. He thought Christ's toes beautiful enough to kiss as he dangled from his cross, graceful, arms outstretched, head to one side, knees together and face sad. Candles flickered like stars about the place, passionate singing filled the air, and all the women in flowing robes were married to that beauty on the cross. But the worshipped figure had another significance too. It was the only reference Eban had to his own sex. He thought him the only other male in all the world and felt special.

Eban September was drawn to the theatre of Catholicism like a bee to pollen. The icons especially intrigued him. One was of a child enveloped in golden robes. In his left hand rested an orb, also gold, with a pearl cross on top of it. On his head he wore a crown so precious Eban felt sure that it must be worth more than any other thing.

"Isn't he a little prince?" came Sister Helen's warm Irish tones close to his small soft ear one morning as he gazed. Eban nodded.

After that, he asked more about princes and kings and royalness. Kind Sister Helen told him whatever she knew about them. Their dogs and their palaces and their lands and their clothes and their horses and their riches. The tales were whispered in snippets for fear that Sister Lara or Sister Dawn would hear and go telling Mother Superior all about it. But the secretive way the stories were told only enhanced their appeal, and morning noon and night Eban prayed to God and Jesus and princes.

At thirteen Eban felt himself becoming other. Men were not allowed in the convent. So the grown child gave himself just ten more nights in heaven. He cried through each of them, then on the last night, when all God's wives were sleeping, he went to the chapel, took a vow of celibacy just as his sweet sisters had done and wandered away from that place forever.

Soon enough Eban realised there were other men, in the mountains and beyond. He saw what men did and felt sad that he was one of them. He thanked God for making him a different colour at least, darker, which he hoped would indicate to one and all that he was made of kinder stuff. Instead people feared him, rejected him, were suspicious of him. He felt sorry that they were so confused.

Eban never showed any outward signs of being religious. Never went to church, never prayed in public, never carried a Bible. Not even Thomas knew about his friend's faithful background or noble vow. Eban believed faith to be a matter for his insides.

Because he found most people too cruel to live happily amongst one another, Eban chose to remain apart. Years of isolation made him talk to himself. He cut words short, jumbled them up and said them backwards. After all, he knew what came next and understood well enough what he meant. But the chatter became a habit and after a while be forgot how to move his tongue any other way around his thoughts. It alienated him further still, and if his skin hadn't concealed him so well in the dark he would have been strung up for his unholy babbling many times.

The suppleness of all babies' limbs was something that never left Eban September's. He enjoyed the feeling of what his body could do. In his body he felt his spirit, felt his God, and he knew that He would not have made him that way – black and limber as a cat – for no good reason.

He performed his own brand of dance unselfconsciously, almost involuntarily. When it was time to take a break from the work he shouldered with Thomas, he would often dance rather than rest. The older man would sit on the ground and laugh, more with pleasure than amusement, and nod subtle encouragement to his friend. Thomas never asked what the moves meant or why Eban made them, he just knew that it was good.

News of the royal train reached Eban by chance. A couple, relaxing down by the Olifants River of a Sunday afternoon, were discussing the event as he crouched behind them, undetected. "If I make myself a bright yellow dress, then the prince might notice me better," said the girl. The words shot through Eban like a light, and a vision came to him at once. He rushed passed the startled lovers, down to the water and pushed his head under so that he could see more clearly. The hallucination showed him dancing in front of the little golden prince. The detail was so clear and the movements were slowed down to better help him remember. In the vision the little prince was so awestruck by the ebony creature with bendy limbs that he dropped his precious orb and clapped his small chubby hands.

It was this very dance which Eban practiced in anticipation of the prince's visit. It was full of impossible balances and peculiar contortions but he recalled the vision a thousand times and eventually mirrored the shapes exactly.

Four months into Eban's stay at De Rust, Mary Eland saw the dance whilst spying on him, as she did frequently. She swooned and wondered how much longer she could remain sober and ordered. Her passion overwhelmed her and she slunk off to the bedroom to be alone a while.

Money

While Sara de Beer spent much of her time trying to skate around the house, clinging to a seething Anne Sutton, her husband was generally to be found at Larry's Saloon gambling, or Rosie Botha's place cavorting, or sweet-talking bank manager Patrick Bloomfield mainly because of the gambling.

Rich Larry was nicknamed at the age of forty. He had been Oudtshoorn's least popular butcher before that and was most often called by his surname: Trutter. Trutter loved to bore his customers with tales of his poverty. It was a topic he considered more interesting than birth or death or flood or drought. "Do you know what the rent is on this place? Huh? Go on, have a guess," he'd say. And the new grandmother or recently widowed would be forced into volunteering a variety of prices. "No. ..No. ..No. ..You'll never get it," he'd say, then announce the figure and follow up with a tedious explanation as to why it was that he had so little money. The lazy wife and the thankless children. If it weren't for them he would undoubtedly be rich. "Rich!" Trutter had plenty of wonderful ideas, but no support for any of them: goat fur hats, cufflinks made from sheep hooves, a file you attached to your thumb as a pencil sharpener. Ironically, it was one of his supposedly unsupportive wife's ideas that finally did make Larry Trutter a very wealthy man.

Lolly Trutter (the wife) had cunningly suggested they raffle a ham in an attempt to raise funds enough to marry off their eldest, none too pretty, daughter. The parents were so pleased at the prospect of finally being rid of 'the ugly one' that they were keen to award the husband a generous dowry but could not afford it.

Customers and even just passers-by were fascinated by the ham. Some bought almost enough tickets to have purchased outright the identical gammon displayed beside it. But it was the ham with a broad white ribbon strapped about it and "Wedding Raffle Ham" signage pronged into its rind that bewitched them, and within a week the nett profit from the raffle had soared to seven hundred per cent.

The day the ham finally found its lucky owner the shop filled more than half an hour before the actual giveaway and Larry Trutter had to solicit the help of policeman Niels Hammon (three tickets clutched in his right hand) to help move everyone outside.

Thirty minutes later a crowd of about sixty ticket holders and another hundred spectators had gathered in the main street. Traffic was blocked but nobody minded, they just joined the crowd. In the twenty minutes before the giveaway a further forty tickets were sold and when the great moment came the Trutters were sure of a one-thousand per cent profit on the hunk of pig.

On a sturdy table in the middle of Main Street, Lolly Trutter and her ugly daughter held the ham aloft while Larry plucked the winning number from a hat. The winner was a poor farm labourer called Dorrie Niemand who fainted when her number was called and had to recover in the shade with her head resting upon the prize a while before she could manage it home.

Later that same day, the father of the bride poured a little of the profits down his throat at The Wagon Wheel bar. Elated by the bonanza, he claimed the idea of the raffle as his own and decided to expand on the concept: "If people will pay, and pay, in the hopes of winning a bloody ham, then imagine what they will pay if the prize is a pile of cash! We saw it today, Oudtshoorners are gamblers. The whole bloody lot of you! And I am going to be your friend."

The local law was easily bribed and within a year Larry's casino had made him a millionaire.

Thys de Beer's predicament was not unique. Trips abroad,

English educations for their children, furs, jewellry, furniture. Oudtshoorn's wealthy denied themselves nothing and most were hugely in debt to the bank, which extended credit based on as much as a six month projected income. But for gamblers, like the mayor, even this was no longer sufficient.

He'd make it all back. He just needed a little time, and anyway, who was he to beg? He was the wealthiest man in a town full of millionaires.

Action

$\mathscr{S}$ince the departure of his poor bloated wife, bank manager Patrick Bloomfied had undergone a significant transformation. Never one for extravagance he became almost obsessed with his appearance and spent especially huge sums on shoes. The dandy inside him had become the dandy about him, and his attire was impossible to ignore.

Agatha Teeling-Smith took particular interest in monitoring his look, and being the town's greatest trendsetter, it soon became a popular pastime among many bored Oudtshoorners. Agatha would say: "Eyes left!" or "Eyes right!" or "Full Bloom at eleven o'clock!" mostly to Nessie Plaatjies who most often accompanied her to town. Nessie who never quite got the hang of this coded speech, would invariably start investigating her madam's left or right eye with whatever hand was not full of parcel. Or look about for a public clock that might display the hour. Of course it ruined any covert staring possibilities and desperate for companionship in her observations, Agatha resorted to hissing, prodding, and very often pointing directly at the bank manager before Nessie understood. Then the indiscretion peaked. Giggling, thigh-slapping, squealing and parcel-dropping were not unusual. The Coiffured One was often upon them by then and Agatha would have to greet the man more effusively than was natural in order to smother her maid's emissions. "Marvellous morning Bloomfield. Absolutely magnificent wouldn't you say?! Just breathe that air!"

Unlike her more extravagant contemporaries, Agatha had been under no obligation to the bank manager and had therefore offered him little more than a clipped "Morning," or "Afternoon". But with the death of his wife and the birth of his style things had changed, and the adjustment in her manner led Bloomfield to conclude that Agatha harboured a burning affection for him. This thought sparked panic in his mouth and made him stammer whenever they met: "Ah ... Yes ... Ah ah a...a...a...absolutely m...m...maam." Because his flustering began at around the same time his wife had passed away and his wardrobe had swelled, Agatha believed Patrick Bloomfield was repressing a gamut of special feelings for her. "The man is a mess!" she'd tell Nessie once they'd moved on. "Did you see the way he almost tipped that hideous hat right off the top of his head when he greeted me. Waf! It's ridiculous. Imagine a woman like me taking any romantic interest in a man like that."

Agatha wasn't the only thing that was making Patrick Bloomield increasingly nervous. Cash flow was down to a trickle in Oudtshoorn but the lending continued to gush. What if there was a crash like before? Well, the bank would just import a herd of bailiffs from George and Port Elizabeth to seize everyone's belongings. And what about him? Well, he'd have to leave town.

The ease with which the ostrich farmers had made their money afforded the stuff little respect. Like spoiled children they thought it might as well have grown on trees. The fact that it came out of birds' backsides meant it was all the same to them. People spent money just to show that they could. One man bought all the train tickets for a round trip from Oudtshoorn to George so that he could ride the train alone and not have it stop at any of the stations along the way. There was a woman who had made a fortune distributing feathers in Europe who staged a full dress rehearsal of her own funeral in her back garden, even though she was not ill. She paid two hundred people three shillings each to attend. There was a chamber orchestra playing her favourite pieces by Johann Sebastian Bach, and a luxurious, satin-lined coffin was actually entombed.

The not-yet deceased directed proceedings from the vantage of a specially built platform and shouted her orders through a loud-hailer. "More heart in the singing! More tears! Drop your heads more! No, not like that, I can still see too many chins!" and so on.

The money made people crazy. Pierrot troupes, ballet concerts, and roller-skates were the least of it. With nobody checking themselves, the bank finally took action, and Standard Bank Headquarters issued a letter making it plain that further lending to those who were hugely overdrawn was to stop until the deficit shrank.

And so, Patrick Bloomfield, though certainly taken aback, was not surprised to see Thys de Beer sweating through his cream coloured linen suit, puffing energetically at a cigar and flapping at his thigh with a folded copy of the *Oudtshoorn Sun* when he entered his office after lunch one Wednesday.

He tried to remember how many times he had consumed at least ten pounds worth of food and liquor at the good table de Beer? Fifteen? Thirty? De Beer, the man who had always been a tolerant host to his disgraceful departed wife. "I don't care what the others say, I like Isadora," he told Bloomfield once as they carried her into the conservatory so that she could sober up more discreetly after an unfortunate tussle with a cherub-encrusted plinth and a vase of proteas, "I like her. She really goes for it," he'd said.

Now here he sat, hot, dishevelled, and slightly drunk, in the manager's office at two o'clock on a Wednesday afternoon. For the first time Bloomfield noticed that de Beer was quite fat. "I've just realised," started the visitor without looking round on hearing Bloomfield's soft leather step behind him, "I've never been in your office." De Beer shrugged out a laugh, "Always done business in more friendly surroundings. My home, or the club. A handshake – that type of thing." Bloomfield froze behind the speaker. The moment was rank with significance. Tragedy loomed thick as the heat. The desk fan whirred and Bloomfield moved towards it in search of relief, but as he got there de Beer noticed the whirring too and turned the propeller to face him. "Afternoon Thys, what a surprise," ventured Bloomfield trying to sound light and optimistic. He removed his burgundy panama, adjusted his pale green cravat, sat down and attempted a smile.

"Yes, I'm surprised too," shot back de Beer suddenly becoming savage, "Surprised that you have the heart to face my beloved Sara when she passes you in the street!" Then without pausing, "What the hell do you call this?" He tossed a note without an envelope towards the man who had sent it. The fan scooped it sideways a moment then let it drop to the floor. Unfazed because of the liquor, de Beer bent forward, retrieved the letter and clutched it aloft. The letter had been Bloomfield's brainwave, a brilliant idea, a way of letting everyone know the credit was curbed without having to engage each overspent farmer face to face. But now here he was, face to face with the most spent of the lot and it was not pretty. "Well Patrick, are you going to insult me further or are you going to give me the cash?"

De Beer left the Standard Bank with the only currency Rich Larry liked, being as he was shrewder and greedier than any provincial bank manager.

Loser

That same week, the de Beer children returned to England after the Christmas break, where they would continue to learn how to behave as little like their forefathers as possible.

It had been a terrible time for everyone. The two young de Beers despised their parents' crude manners and basic language which made Thys all the crasser and their mother all the shakier – which in turn made her all the more ridiculous. The children became increasingly disdainful, which made the father more gross – and so on.

That night after the debacle at the bank, Anne Sutton, to whom Sara generally extended an invitation to dine with her and her husband, had retired to her room with a tray of supper, suffering, she said, from a migraine brought on by the horrible African sun. And so Sara and Thys de Beer ate alone. Sara noticed at once that her husband was not quite as pleased with himself as usual, but she decided not to dwell on his mood for fear that it might influence her own which was buoyant.

"Thys," she gushed, the moment the soup slid before them, "I've had a brilliant idea."

"Hmnm."

"I'm already getting them made."

De Beer, having lined Rich Larry's pockets with the money he had prised out of Patrick Bloomfield not two hours earlier, was in no mood for enthusiasm let alone ambiguity. "You'll never guess what they are," chirped his wife.

"No, I'll never bloody guess! What? What?" shouted Thys.

Sara ignored his temper and blurted excitedly: "Real gold roller skates for the prince!"

De Beer had never noticed his wife's extravagance much before as there was simply too much money to care. But now he was enraged. He roared at her for minutes. He smashed his soup spoon down so violently that chicken and vegetables leapt from the bowl and spewed at the linen. Then he clenched both his fists and hammered on the table. "... And besides all that you stupid bloody woman," he went, "How do you think the prince is going to glide gracefully about on skates that weigh ten pounds a piece!"

Sara sobbed. She'd never seen her husband lose his temper before. He hardly ever raised his voice at all in anger. She tried to explain that the skates were only gold plated, but confessed she'd never thought about how much they might weigh. But de Beer stopped her. He wasn't finished yet. He told her how for nearly thirty years her voice, ideas, laugh, friends had all driven him mad. Mad! Then he declared their offspring to be a bunch of spoiled English brats, and even Anne Sutton's eyes had clearly lost their appeal for he referred to her as a hoity-toity pain in the neck who he had to restrain himself from throttling every time he saw her! Then he stood up and had a heart attack.

It was not fatal. The mayor recovered well and a large part of his convalescence was spent stroking the hand of his beloved Sara and telling her how he hadn't meant the wicked things he'd said, not even the part about Anne Sutton, and that he was just an old fool who didn't deserve such a wonderful wife. Sara forgave him happily, nursed him lovingly and sent Anne Sutton back to England. She felt she could manage her personality by herself now.

Escape

As Angel splashed cold water on the sore, bruised place between her legs, Van der Want lounged on his verandah and enjoyed the tingling in his balls. He basked in the solitude of evil and swiped at his youngest son when he brought him a cup of coffee, thereby disturbing his recall. Jabbing at that screaming girl out there in the field. Nobody coming to help her. Everybody petrified by his supreme savagery. His penis swelled again at the thought, so he fished it out and masturbated casually into the evening air.

Tomorrow he would go and get some more.

The next day, afraid to be alone, Angel went to the mill with her parents. Van der Want suspected as much and made his way there directly. He stood in the entrance, his bulk shutting out most of the light, plunging the interior into appropriate gloom. The frightened family stopped their work. "Come," said Van der Want, gesturing. Angel didn't look at her parents for fear of involving and thereby endangering them. She walked towards the monster, each step hurting. Three, sometimes four times a week Van der Want found Angel and did that thing to her again. Angel never had time to heal properly and the pain only grew less because she was becoming so very numb.

Hannes deteriorated rapidly. He went to bed at night and wept like a baby, and his eyes were perpetually red from all the crying he did. When Ruth wasn't consoling him she was trying to soothe her daughter, who was becoming increasingly distant.

"You must go to De Rust," said Ruth to Angel one night over

supper about month into the relentless assault. "It's too far for you to walk alone, and if we all leave he'll easily see us and bring us back, and then I don't know what. So I'll put you on the train. " The plan seemed ridiculous. Van der Want lived not a hundred yards from from the railway siding. "We'll put you on from the other side of the track, the side away from the house. "

"But how will I get there without him seeing?"

Hannes started to weep and groan: Van der Want would kill them all. Van der Want would eat them up! His mouth hung open and the half chewed bread inside plopped out in doughy gobs down his shirt-front. Ruth and Angel stroked his arms and continued. "We'll borrow Kobus's mule and cart and load it with lucerne and hide you underneath it. Then we'll stop the cart at the track and when the train pulls in you can jump on quickly. "

"How will we know when the train is due? It never comes at the same time and if we wait there with the cart, Van der Want will come to ask what we're doing."

"Sweepie's boys, Stefan and Saagie, they'll put their ears to the track. They can always tell when the train is coming. "

The attempt failed. Ben Isaac saw the whole thing. The girl jumped out of the lucerne and pulled herself up onto the train. As she did so, Van der Want, who had noticed the cart near the track, started down his six front steps, waving his gun and shouting to Ben Isaac not to leave the siding yet.

Innocent Ben waited while Van der Want sauntered down the track towards him. Van der Want walked around the train, taking his time. He grabbed the reins of Kobus's mule and stood there shouting for Angel to get off the train. Angel found the guard and clung to him. She begged him not to make her go, that this man was going to kill her if he did. The guard hesitated. "Ben! " called Van der Want over his shoulder. "Tell your guard to push her off. She's a thief. She's trying to escape."

"It's not true!" pleaded Angel.

Ben was speechless. The guard hesitated, then prised Angel's grip from his arm and lowered her down to Van der Want.

"Okay Ben! You can go."

The train chugged slowly away, Van der Want turned and watched it go, gripping Angel with his left hand, the reins in his right.

Nobody was directly punished that day. Van der Want just kept hurting Angel like before and knew that it would be enough to kill the lot of them in the end.

Guilt

Ben Isaac had seen a lot of things in his time. Glimpses of inhumanity twinkled up at him from the grass either side of the track, usually miles from a stop of any kind, and with the engine at full steam there was nothing he could do about it. But this. Should he have helped the girl away to a safer place? She didn't look like a thief, she looked more like an angel. Would Van der Want really kill her? He thought about it alone for a week before he told Hannah. His sweetheart advised him to either confront Van der Want or forget about it. Anything else seemed pointless and would only force him into an early grave and then where would she be without a husband and not much of a pension? And with her mother dead. And with no children. And all alone. Where would it leave her?

Ben thought these options over, but the picture he got of himself confronting the giant was too frightening for him to look at even in his mind's eye, and forgetting about the girl with copper hair was just too hard. "Hannah!" he exclaimed one morning the moment he opened his eyes and before Hannah had a chance to open hers. "I know what to do!"

"About what?"

"About Van der Want and the girl."

"What?"

"I'm going to report it to the police. Let them deal with it."

Later that same day, during his lunch break, Ben made his way to the police station in George. He believed in the police. Believed that they were there to see justice done, the people's friend and all that.

When he entered the police station, he approached a group of five of the good Samaritans in black and slowly told them the tale. A young constable scribbled it all down and read it back to him, and the sergeant assured him that they would look into the matter. As Ben was leaving, he heard them laughing. He hesitated a moment, then decided they must be sharing a good joke about another matter and kept walking away, happy to have finally done the right thing.

Visions

*T*homas was dying. The only opinion regarding his state of health which he could afford had been that of a travelling quack who said he thought he was probably suffering from tuberculosis and that he would die whether he went to hospital or not. Thomas kept working until he hardly had the strength to stand and after that Eban would carry him outside whenever he wanted to look at the sky and then carry him back in again to rest. Evenings, his friend would sit and feed him and tell him how work on the farm was going. Mary hovered not entirely without sympathy, though hardly distraught and she tried to appear more upset than she really was because she wanted to impress Eban.

One week before Thomas finally drifted off to sleep for the last time, he woke with a terrible fear. He shouted out and became uncharacteristically panicked. Eban heard and rushed from the other room to tend the commotion. He held his friend who raved incomprehensibly and asked him to speak more slowly. Thomas tried:

"There is an angel and it's terrible. Terrible!" Eban looked at his friend, now so frail, and concluded that he was hallucinating, being as he was so close to death. He thought about the nuns. He thought about their idea of heaven, their icons, the imagery surrounding death, or rather life eternal.

"Don't eb afrid. It's no'terbl, It's 'ust Hevn."

"No! it's not heaven, it's real. The angel is hurting. She is so sore."

Thomas sobbed and mumbled a while more before falling asleep, exhausted, sad, a frown on his face.

Next morning early, Ruth burst through her brother's front door. Mary didn't recognise her at first and asked what the hell she thought she was doing, busting into her house like that, and reached for a broom to beat her outside with. Mary had been so drunk when Ruth had lived there, she hardly remembered her at all. Too distressed to indulge the idiot, Ruth pushed past her and into Thomas's room. There she found Eban September sitting on the floor next to the bed, praying. Then she saw her small yellow brother and fell to her knees, crying and kissing his hands and face and repeating his name and her name over and over. Thomas opened his eyes, which also wept, and he knew at once that his ghoulish visions of the night before had something to do with her coming.

They talked a long time. It was as if Thomas took the days he had left and condensed a week's worth of breath into that conversation. Eban moved in and out of the room, with buckets of piss and cups of coffee. Mary soon lost interest in it all and fell asleep on Eban's mat in the hopes that he might join her when he was tired.

As Ruth's tale unravelled, the air became fogged with the horror of it. Thomas's tears kept coming. Eban listened without blinking. Van der Want was right, his ritual abuse of Angel was killing the parents as well as the girl. Hannes hardly worked any more, and Angel never smiled. Ruth was sure the two of them were going mad and knew that if she sat and watched, passive, much longer, that she would have no option but to join them. It had taken Ruth fifty hours to reach her old home. Before she left Vlakteplaas, she issued a few simple instructions to the catatonic pair. "Angel, I'm going to get help. Do you understand me? I'm going to get my brother, Thomas. Angel, keep going with Van der Want until I get back and if he asks where I am, tell him I'm ill. Look after Pappie while I'm away. Will you do that for me?"

Angel hardly cried any more, she just stared at her mother, her face blank and afraid, and said nothing. Hannes understood well enough what Ruth had said and began to protest noisily. No words, just groaning and tears and frantic rocking to and fro in his customary hunched position on the floor. Angel kept staring at her mother. Even when Ruth embraced her and became fuzzy, out of focus because she was too close, she did not move her eyes.

Eban September was so moved by Ruth's horrible chronicle he thought of nothing else the whole of the next day. Rich images accompanied his thoughts and the beautiful olive-skinned girl with Titian hair began to haunt him. In his mind she was like the little prince of gold and by the time his work was over that day, Eban had resolved to kill Van der Want.

Hate

*L*eaving Thomas on his death bed was the hardest thing either Ruth or Eban had ever had to do. He looked so small when they said goodbye. He looked like an old woman. But Thomas urged them to go back before Angel was hurt any more. They knew he was right, so they said goodbye to their dearest and started walking east.

The journey was hazardous. Baboons chased them several times, a cobra reared up at them, a freak cloudburst drenched them and a bloody-minded farmer who caught them crossing his land made them go round his farm's perimeter, thereby stretching their walk by another four miles. It was as if Van der Want had called on Satan to send the plagues. To slow them down. To warn them off. Eban loved Ruth. She was so like her brother. Ruth trusted Eban and for the first time since it started, she thought there might be a way to end the nightmare. Forty hours they trudged with scant sleep and less food. Darkness concealed their approach at Vlakteplaas and they reached Ruth's cottage without being apprehended by Van der Want. The front door stood wide open. Hannes sat on the floor in front of the hearth, scratching lines into his legs with a rusty nail. Ruth gently took the weapon from him, then held him tight. "It's alright. It's alright. I'm here my darling. Shoo, shoo. Hannes my love, where's Angel?" she said. There was no sign of the girl. The demented man with bleeding calves made a whimper which sounded like some insane wind moving through a keyhole. "Shoo, shoo. Did she come home today? Hannes? Did she come home?" Now Hannes wailed like an animal. Trapped, lost.

"It's alright, we have help now my darling. Don't cry. Don't cry any more Hannes. Shoo."

It was a sight so pitiful it made Eban September's black, angular face damp as he watched. Ruth and Hannes clung to each other a long time, each seemingly unwilling to let go first. What for? To feel more frightened? Alone again?

Eban sat on the floor a while, resting his back against the wall, and thought about what he had to do. He realised from Hannes's behaviour that Van der Want had the girl, and the scene of her grieving parents still going on in front of him made the prospect of the task seem not so hard. He would wring the neck, chop the ears, stab the belly of Van der Want. Eban supposed that this was hate.

Killing

$\mathcal{V}$an der Want kept a closer eye on Ruth's family since Angel's attempted escape. Sometimes he would turn up at the cottage at odd hours, demand coffee and rusks and tell the parents how he liked to fuck their daughter. He arrived at their hut only hours after Ruth had left for De Rust, and when he discovered no Ma sick in bed, he had dragged Angel out by her hair and blithely told gibbering Hannes he would never see his girl again. Hannes had been slowly mutilating himself ever since. His arms and legs were torn and bloody all over. By the time Ruth found him, some of his wounds were festering. She bathed them and bound them with strips of her best cotton tablecloth – the one Angel had embroidered when she was a child.

"Wer' is' e?" said Eban suddenly.

Ruth had never asked Eban what he intended to do about Van der Want, but now, just by looking at him, she understood. It was a sin to kill a man, but a demon?

"I'll take you," she said

"No, 'ust tell em."

Ruth walked outside and pointed the way to the house. Then she held the two big, black hands a moment, stared steadily into the watery brown eyes, and turned back inside and dabbed Hannes some more. How to kill a man? Eban didn't know, but his hurried stride gave him only a few minutes before he'd have his victim within reach, then what? Never mind, He'd know what to do. It wouldn't be the first time one man had murdered another using his bare hands without any clear strategy in mind. What a terrible thing, thought Eban.

He wondered how strong Van der Want would be. No matter, God would give him strength. David and Goliath. Where would Angel be? With him? Somewhere else? Dead? Where would the wife be? Would she try to stop him? Maybe not. Ruth had said she was unloved.

The house with the verandah, and broekie lace and six white steps was not locked. Van der Want never dreamed that anyone would dare try to harm him or steal from him so the black cat slipped through the front door, stealthy as a ghost. He padded from one room to the next as deftly as if the light within had been white rather than charcoal. Not the slightest creak or bump did he effect. The first bedroom revealed four lumps in two beds.

One was Erma, but she was so tiny it looked like a lump of child. The next room Eban came to was different. One great berth heaved with the blissful sleep of a creature that must have had lungs the size of blacksmith's bellows and either a clear conscience or none at all – Van der Want. But Eban didn't linger. Where was Angel? After searching he realised that she was not in the house. He went through the unbolted back door and started searching the outbuildings. Goats, just goats everywhere. They'd make a rumpus if he wasn't careful. She must be somewhere among them. He stepped gently through the sleeping animals. Not one stirred, but Angel did. She sensed him somehow, as if being chained up like a dog had sharpened her senses: hearing and smell. She could sniff out a man among beasts and she knew this wasn't Van der Want. Van der Want smelled like the dead.

"Shk, shk," she went

Eban froze at the sound.

"Shk," she spat again. He was sure he was the only phantom in the place and knew it must be Angel. He moved fervently towards the call until he found her, chained to the wall at the far end of the shed.

"I 'il fre oyu," he said.

"But Van der Want has the keys."

"At's s ri'ght. I 'il fre oyu."

Then Eban made his way lightly, back through the goats.

In Van der Want's room Eban stood watching the blankets surge and subside. The mass which had wheezed before, now snored tremendously. From where he stood near the door, all Eban could see of the rapist was the matted black hair, not yet flecked with grey the way it should have been, had it been of human growth.

Eban walked around the bed to check the face of the thing he was about to kill. He was spared the satanic stare, the eyes shut away in deep, muddy sockets. The fat chapped lips shuddered each time the wind roared past the tombstone teeth and the fragrant Karoo night air was exhaled foul smelling as rotting flesh and the pillow absorbed the spit which drooled like venom with every sigh.

Eban moved back to the other side of the bed again. What to do now? He would seize the neck from behind, no, he wanted to see that face as it died. He must climb on top and pin down the body using the weight of his own and throttle him that way.

Now there really was a ghost, a shrivelled woman in a white night gown, long thin hair the same colour as her shift, and a face no darker but for the birthmark along her jaw. Eban was petrified. He was already on top of the still sleeping Van der Want, hands outstretched, ready to strangle. But Erma just stood there, staring a moment. Then she nodded, impatient for the intruder to get on with it. Eban looked down at Van der Want and thought about dear Ruth, bleeding Hannes, raped Angel, dying Thomas. The thoughts grew bloodier. He imagined Van der Want's huge penis, ripping into Angel, his hands pulling savagely at her breasts, the teeth biting the nipples – almost off – enjoying the feeling of her vagina contracting in pain around him.

Eban grabbed the huge, muscular neck, his hands, so lean and graceful which had struck so many magical poses, clamped brutally onto skin, muscle, sinew. Van der Want's eyes shot open. He growled and spat. His body thrashed like some hooked giant fish. The bedding was kicked loose and Eban had to lean heavier on the chest of bellows and grip hard with his knees to keep from sliding to the floor with the sheets.

Within seconds the battle began to turn. Van der Want puffed his neck out somehow, allowing some air to pass down his throat. He pulled his arms out from under Eban's thighs and began prising the hands away from his neck. The killer kept pushing down and tried to imagine Van der Want no tougher than a chicken, but he was losing strength. Van der Want's hands were now around Eban's neck. Eban knew he would die, but what about Angel?

Suddenly Van der Want let out an incredible scream. It seemed it would never end. But it did, and his grip slacked off Eban. Seconds passed before Eban realised his victim had stopped moving. The eyes were still open and the fetid breath still came, though thinner than before, but he was as good as dead: limp, passive. Eban stayed there a minute. His grip had relaxed but his hands remained at the neck. Then the awful eyes slowly closed and the breath thinned to nothing, and Van der Want was dead.

Eban remembered the spook at the door and looked round for it. There was nothing there. He then noticed a warm wetness in the seat of his pants and as he twisted to look he saw Erma, behind him now, at the foot of the bed, holding her husband's penis in one hand and a kitchen knife in the other.

Shame

The white folks at De Rust had never been so happy. The prince was coming in just ten days. Everyone's outfits were sewn. Everyone's hair styles perfected. Ironically, the man largely responsible for their excitement was too upset to enjoy any of it.

Rosa had sought no sympathy for her bashed face, and most locals offered none. Defending a black man and embarrassing her husband in public was just plain shameful. There were some who thought she'd got off too lightly.

"I'd have killed her!"

"I'd have cut out her tongue!"

"I'd have kicked her out of the house there and then!" raged the husbands on and on. Their wives responded like nervous children in a playground, watching the school bully twist a smaller child's nose – so pleased their men were not angry at them that they resisted any association with the injured. A couple of kindly souls consoled her, Hettie Botha among them, but on the whole Rosa was snubbed.

The Prinsloos themselves didn't talk about it. They hardly addressed each other at all any more. But Rosa wasn't playing her part right. The disgraced was meant to cower, flinch, try desperately to please. Instead she seemed to become bolder, as if her act of courage had tasted so sweet that she kept licking at it.

The status quo in the household was cause for much speculation in the village. Did Rosa love the kaffir, or was she just insane? Would there be a divorce, and if so, who would run the shop that sold everything? Surely not the wife. Karel had never wondered too much about love. When he met Rosa she was nineteen and something to behold. Tall, voluptuous, brunette. Big brown eyes, full red lips and the kind of tits he liked to give a good squeeze.

Her family was not so humble as his own. Rosa had learned to read and write better than he. But this sudden interest in art, and more importantly artists, what was that? Yes, they had a few pictures, prints, that Rosa hung about the place, and there was a book she'd bought once on a trip to George, *The Story of Painting*, but Karel hadn't thought anything of it. If Rosa had been obsessed with such things, he would have noticed.

No, she'd been a good wife to him, and mother to their four children, all grown now, all moved too far away to visit much anymore. Of course he loved her. Something had to happen, and it did. When Karel returned home after a long, hard Saturday afternoon, chatting and drinking down by the track, he found a note. He had seen his wife keeping shop as usual that morning, even helped her out a bit. After that, he'd joined his usual drinking cronies at the track, and by dusk the liquor had softened his resolve to punish Rosa Prinsloo forever. She probably hadn't meant anything by defending the kaffir, she was just cranky perhaps. The whole thing had been blown out of proportion. He'd go home and tell her he forgave her then kiss her and grab those wonderful tits.

But when he arrived home that night there were no lips to kiss, no breasts to fondle, just a note:

> *Dear Karel*
> *I am sorry for everything. I don't love the black*
> *dancer, but I did love a black man once before. It*
> *was a long time ago, before I met you. He was a*
> *man who worked for my parents. He was as black*
> *as that one, and I loved him.*
> *He never touched me, but I knew he loved me too.*

*Please keep this a secret I am going to our daughter
Letta for a while.
I hope you enjoy the prince.*

Rosa

It took Karel a while to read the note. His eyes weren't all that good and neither was his reading, but he understood it well enough after a while and it made him sick to his stomach. He stormed about the house, furious, tormented, and gave volume to his thoughts. This couldn't be! Life was not so dramatic. His life was never so. Mostly it had gone smoothly. They went to church. They never missed it! Rosa was well loved among the good ladies of the Dutch Reformed congregation. She helped organise wonderful fêtes and picnics. She loved the church! Everything was nice and normal. Decent!

His lascivious thoughts of earlier sprang to mind and made him gag. He hung his head over the blue enamel basin and panted. The whore. The disgusting whore. Keep it a secret PAH! He would tell everyone! He would tell the whole world that she loved a kaffir!

He told no one.

Missing

$\mathcal{E}$ban, Erma and Angel shovelled a ton of dirt that night, impatient to bury the brute. All of them were weak with hunger, yet somehow they mustered the stamina. The boys, Van der Want's sons, wakened by their father's last scream, made coffee and burned sheets.

When the sun came up that morning, Vlakteplaas was beautiful for the first time in seventeen years. But the day highlighted more practical issues too, like what to tell the police. Erma smiled slightly and said she knew of a story which had worked well once before.

She waited three days then sent an anxious note to the police in Uniondale by way of Ben Isaac.

> *Dear Mr Hanekom*
> *My husband, Pieter van der Want of Vlakteplaas is*
> *missing. Three days.*
> *He never leaves the farm and nobody says they*
> *have seen him.*
> *I sent my sons to look but they only find his horse*
> *nothing else.*
> *Please help.*
>
> *Erma van der Want*

Frik Hanekom allocated just one man to skim the area, but disappearances of that sort in a vastness of that sort were not uncommon: a lot of leopard in the hills. Besides, Van der Want was becoming a liability. Judge Bull was dead and the new man of justice was just that. So Hanekom was not about to send a team of men to start digging around Vlakteplaas. They might turn up more than one body.

Erma was less nervous about the murder than the others. She showed neither fear nor remorse, and now that she was allowed to unleash it, the extent of her dementia became clearly apparent. She laughed at nothing and sang loudly in a voice better suited to flat frightened whispers. She yelled at insects, then smashed them flat, and she caressed her sons as if they were lovers.

The boys either engrossed themselves in their chores or played more boisterously than before. They became louder – too loud, and rougher by the day. Their excitement had a menacing edge to it. Their mother disconcerted rather than scared them. As for Pappie, well, they tried to forget.

The labourers and tenants observed from a distance and noted Van der Want's increasing absence with anticipation and as time passed, a growing sense of relief. The devil's well-being was hardly their concern, it was the possibility that he might return that kept them tense. Just as they had found no brother of Pieter van der Want all those years before, so the police found no Pieter van der Want now. Three months after the killing, Erma received his death certificate by way of post.

Eban's Heart

The Willemses remained at Vlakteplaas a while for fear of rousing suspicion. Eban remained just two days. He was keen to get back to Thomas. It was a strange forty-eight hours. Nobody worked, they just stayed around the cottage, dazed by the nightmare past. By the peace. Eban was ambivalent about what he had done. Had he killed Van der Want or had Erma? Was he a sinner or a saint? He imagined conversations with the nuns about it. They would know. But the images he got were always of the Sisters crossing themselves and shaking their heads. They were telling him he was wrong. And yet he didn't feel bad. If he hadn't killed Van der Want then Van der Want would eventually have killed Angel. It was the lesser of two evils.

Eban was infatuated with Angel. As he made her out that fateful night in the gloom of that stinking shed, chained and bloody, he was more enchanted with her than he had been with any woman before. The circumstances were horrendous, the smell sickening, her hair matted, her clothes spattered with blood and shit, but still she was the most beautiful thing he had ever seen. Since that night Angel did little more than sit quietly or touch her parents lightly. She touched Eban too, once or twice, and thanked him. For the first time, Eban felt embarrassed about the way he spoke and he avoided saying anything during his stay there.

Silence became a theme in the household. "There's been enough silence in this house now," said Ruth softly during supper, thirty-six hours after the killing. "Even Eban has stopped his funny jabbering."

She laughed to ensure that the guest felt loved rather than mocked by the tease. Then everyone started to laugh. It was a rare sound in that valley. Even Hannes was jolly, but when Ruth seized the opportunity to get her husband talking, he stopped at once, looked down at his porridge and was quiet some more. When Eban said goodbye to Angel, he felt the same way he had when he left the convent. Cold. Alone. She could never love him, he was too black and people hated that. (Eban wondered how Rosa Prinsloo was.) True, Angel kissed him when he departed, but that didn't mean anything, she was just polite, grateful to him for killing her molester.

Eban didn't like thinking about Angel. It hurt his head and poked roughly at his chest. He tried to distract himself with thoughts of Thomas, but every five seconds or so she was back with him. He even tried recalling the gory events of three nights earlier, and prayed to his sweet Jesus to forgive him, but in the midst of anxious appeal, Angel's face appeared. The look of it thrilled him. The look of it hurt him. Eban supposed this was love.

Mary's Heart

It was close to an hour past midnight when Eban reached Thomas's cottage. It was cold. The temperature had dropped drastically in the last couple of days, perhaps because the world was rid of one of hell's disciples. The interior was very dark. No fire glowed in the hearth. No candle flickered elsewhere.

"Ma'y? Thoms?" called Eban and pushed the bedroom door aside. The room reeked of sweat and liquor, on the bed Eban made out the figures of Thomas and Mary. He bent down and whispered to Thomas, "Thoms. Thoms jit's Ebn. Thomas, I kl'd th' nam. Angel jis saf' nw. Thoms, Thoms, jit's Ebn. "

Then Eban took his friend's hand. It was stiff and cold. Eban's crying roused Mary from her stupor. It felt as if all the sadness of all his life was coming out of him right then. Mary clumsily tried to hold him and joined in the sobbing. Eban threw her off and demanded to know how long Thomas had been dead. She couldn't say, but she was upset because she had been there all alone with him. "Why were you so long Eban? ! Why?" she asked.

It had been too much for her to bear sober and so now she was drunk and had lost track of time.

"I don't know how long he's been dead. Maybe one day, Maybe two."

Before the night Eban killed a man, he had never hurt a soul, now he felt like he might kill Mary too. He picked her up and shut her out in the cold. Then he washed Thomas Eland's stiff-as-a-plank body and arranged him as best he could.

Mary made so much noise that Eban let her back in after not too long, but he wouldn't let her near Thomas. He ordered her to make a fire and some coffee, but he fell asleep on the floor next to his friend before the water had boiled.

When Eban awoke the next morning, he had the smell of cadaver in his nostrils and he rushed outside for air. The sky hung heavy with storm clouds and a spiteful wind scooped up the dust and flicked it painfully at him. Mary was nowhere, but Eban didn't care. He walked back inside, snatched a blanket off the mattress, pulled it tight around his shoulders and made his way up to Lategan's farmhouse to arrange a funeral for his friend. Eban dug the hole, wrapped the body and delivered a jumbly sermon to good farmers Lategan and bad wife Mary. He filled the grave with earth and peppered it with dried petals he had collected and which the wind wasted no time in scattering across the veld once more.

Mary cried noisily and tried to elicit sympathy from Eban: "My husband is dead! What will happen to me now?! Nobody loves me, nobody cares about me Eban. Eban you must help me." But Eban seemed oblivious of her presence. He spent most of two whole days at the graveside. He prayed and tried to dance but for the first time found this mode of expression was not open to him. He just sat, and lay and walked nearby. Each day Mary would appear more than once and try to get Eban's attention. If the weeping widow didn't work, she'd become the demented banshee. When Eban didn't flinch she'd leave and return fifteen minutes later: the pious griever.

At dawn on the third day the sliver of patience Mary possessed ran out and she launched herself at the sleeping Eban who lay the same way up as they had positioned Thomas's corpse, one arm stretched out a little towards the mound of earth as if to rest on his friend's arm if he had been six feet closer to the sky and still breathing.

Mary hit Eban about the head. Eban leapt to his feet. Then she draped herself across his back and shoulders, feet off the ground, her arms wrapped round his neck like some wounded soldier ready to be lifted away for healing. Eban didn't move, he was too lost in his sorrow to register quite what was happening. Slowly she slid round his body to face him. She looked to his eyes for sympathy and spoke.

"Don't leave me Eban," she whimpered over and over. Then Eban said the words she had always wanted to hear, but never dreamed she might: He would not leave her, he would marry her. Mary drank just enough brandy to keep her from shaking through the ceremony. Lategan and his wife attended. The bride wore a baggy cream dress, Ma Lategan's cast-off, and clutched assorted flora, ripped from the veld by the church. She had washed most of herself and her old green scarf kept the excitable hair under control.

If Eban could have conducted the ceremony himself he would have, thereby rendering it as meaningless in the eyes of the law as it was in his own. He felt guilty, marrying a woman who loved him when he did not feel the same. He felt bad for Mary. What was he doing? But by the time he had run Thomas' death-bed plea through his mind once more, he was married.

He wanted to die. He wanted Angel.

It was hell from the start. After a brief stint waving the Bible had not managed to melt Eban's heart Mary started drinking and whoring again. "I have to sin and sell my body because it would never get poked otherwise! You don't love me!" she'd shout. Eban blamed himself. Mary loved Eban enough to want to destroy him. She would destroy herself in the process, but she didn't care. She was born to rot. And so Mary taunted her new husband day and night:

"Like some fairy! Dancing around that way. You've probably never been with a woman in your life, you useless piece of shit!"

Eban slept where he had always slept, by the hearth. Mary had the rickety double bed in the room next door, which she often shared with some passerby.

Outfits

Agatha sought the opinion of Nessie Plaatjies on all matters of a non-intellectual nature. New recepies, new outfits, new friends. The maid's appraisal was crude, her vocabulary limited, but there was nothing wrong with her eye, palate or honesty. Nice. Yuk. Unusual. Too hot. Too fatty. Bitter. Very fancy – such responses were invaluable to Agatha.

There was a loophole in the arrangement however, and if the woman who dusted books but could not read them, and believed in a demon three feet high that sucked your blood during the night unless you stood your bed on bricks – if she ever overstepped the mark regarding a particularly sensitive subject, Agatha wasted no time dismissing the opinion as nothing weightier than that of an illiterate peasant who believed in vampire dwarfs.

"Nessie, I've had a brilliant idea," announced Agatha one morning some months before the prince's arrival, "I'll go to the roller skate fancy dress ball dressed as an ostrich." Nessie surveyed madam through eyes she made into slits and tried to visualise the way madam had taught her to. Agatha continued, all hands and bosom: "I'll have a magnificent skirt of feathers and a tight grey silk top for the neck, and a sort of ostrich head hat, like the one David Rozenthal wore that time he dressed as a chicken at that orphanage do. You know that photograph Nessie, the one in the dining room where I'm dressed as Venus." Nessie laughed a bit then couldn't help speaking: "But a ostrich neck is long and thin," she said gesturing at her torso whilst breathing in hard and stretching upwards. "Ignorant, superstitious half-wit!" flashed through Agtha's mind as she stroked her midriff. "Well, really!" was all she said.

Nessie realised her mistake at once: "But I think it could be nice. People will still get the idea. I like the skirt part and I think that would look beautiful on madam. Especially if we sew sequins on the feathers like little stars. You'll look like a princess."

"The woman's a genius," flashed through Agatha's mind: "Quite!" she said and left the room.

Mates

"You're right, it probably is the greatest honour a driver could wish for, and I can tell you now, the prince will never have had such a good journey in his whole life. I can drive that engine like it was going along on soap. Smooth like that." Jans Jonker was bragging to a group of men in a Port Elizabeth bar on the eve of the eve of the royal trip. "Have you ever ridden a train with me driving?" he challenged the drinkers, being about as sure that they had not as he was that he had a nose on his face.

"Noo, no, nooo, noo," they lowed.

"Well imagine gliding, no, floating, yes, floating in mid-air like a bird, that's how smooth it is."

The Pig and Boar was not a regular haunt of Jans'. He'd been there once some months back, during the day and liked the atmosphere: no women allowed. Not even a barmaid.

This evening was busier than before and hosted a pleasing array of working men, well-built, some young and tanned, who would pat you on the back with their big strong hands if you bought them a drink – which Jans did, several times. Not long into the session, at which he was indisputably the star, having made plenty of friends through his generosity and regal connections, Jans was confident that he could rely on a fair deal of macho embrace before home time and perhaps some thereafter.

There was one young man who enjoyed more free beer than any other that night. His name was Danie Terreblanche. He was quieter than the rest but warmly greeted by the others, obviously a local and

140

well liked. He was tall, broad shouldered, had thick dark hair, parted on one side and his features were chiselled into shapes everyone understood to be handsome. He was about twenty-four years old and wore no wedding band. "Jans Jonker," said Jans Jonker extending his right hand. Danie smiled and took the hand firmly enough to make Jonker swoon slightly. He recovered and got on with more boasts at once: "… Ja, I stopped the train just in time. This much further," gesturing with his chubby hands about a foot apart, "and she'd have been mince-meat." Dramatic pause while he concentrated on suppressing a fart.

"Ag, I should probably have kept going. The stupid bitch, she didn't even wake up when I moved her off the track, she'd had that much to drink. " Then he looked to Danie for approval and smiled as he spoke. His teeth were crooked, his breath was bad. "Stupid bloody women don't know the time of day. They're all the same! I gave her a good kick before I got back on the train, but what's the use."

Jans was full of tales that night. They all featured him in some heroic capacity, or at least the guy who knew better, and they all revolved around the track, as if it was something which could hardly exist without him. Something he pulled out of his pocket and cast across the landscape whenever he needed to drive along it. His fixation was hardly surprising, there was little else in his life to talk about. By the end of the evening, most listeners had either drifted off to another part of the bar or gone home to their wives. It was enough about the railway, enough about Jans Jonker. Even in a town where nothing much happened his boasting became vapid.

Eventually only Danie Terreblanche remained at his side. Perhaps because he was enjoying the free drinks, perhaps because Jans held him permanently in his gaze, and had moved his stool close enough to stretch out his arm and hug the lad round the neck whenever he looked away.

The Pig and Boar closed at twelve. The last patrons trickled out in a thin wavy formation. The drinkers split up outside or wound away in small groups. They mounted their horses with varying degrees of success. One man had them all laughing when he demonstrated how he'd trained his horse to lie down so that he could mount him more easily when drunk. Funny guy. The rest swayed off in various directions on jelly feet.

Jans lingered, hanging onto his new mate for support. When Danie made to leave Jans begged to be walked home, "I don't think I'll make it otherwise," he said. Young Danie was a good sport, besides, the stranger had paid for his own satisfying sense of inebriation. Sure he'd help him home. Jans had only ever been with coloured boys. They were just too poor to refuse a few shillings to let a white man touch them that way. He thought about love, someone to share his hairy life with him, but he knew it would never happen.

"I don't think I'll make it up alone," puffed Jans, waving at the grubby brown staircase of the Birmingham Hotel, notorious shelter of whores, sailors and cockroaches, where he'd been put up for three nights prior to the royal journey at the railway's expense. Danie lugged the drunker man up to his room on the first floor. He helped unlock the door and propelled Jans towards the bed. The driver, not too drunk to miss the opportunity, made sure he fell awkwardly enough to pull his helper down onto the bed with him.

It was a bad year to be homosexual, and the good sport beat fat old Jans Jonker to mush.

More Tragedy

"What do you mean, Jans isn't here?"

"He isn't here. He's in hospital."

"Visiting I hope."

Port Elizabeth's station master, Sakkie Theron, was well known for his dry wit, but once the full story behind Jans Jonker's absence had unravelled, a humour of sand could not have prevented palpitations.

Danie Terreblanche had broken two Jonker ribs, knocked out two Jonker teeth, cracked one Jonker jaw and left the rest of Jonker more swollen than usual.

"That's not the worst of it sir," continued Harry Swart with a glut of morbid excitement.

"Don't tell me he was wearing his railway uniform at the time!" was the worst thing Sakkie Theron could think of at that moment.

"No, he was wearing his own clothes."

"Thank heavens! Well Swart, get on with it." The ticket collector with pimples on his face who'd been bullied into breaking the news to the boss, looked down at his cap, which he kneaded in his hands like stringy dough.

"Well?! For God's sake Swart, what is it?!"

"It's terrible really sir."

" Yes?!"

"Well, someone in the hotel heard what was going on, the beating and everything, and they opened the door – it wasn't locked, and, well, they stopped the bloke that was hurting him like that, pulled him off and everything, but then the bloke who was doing the beating said something to the other one and then he started kicking him too. Jonker, kicking Jonker, not the other one. Then they took some of the blood, because there was quite a lot of blood, and they wrote something on the wall with it. Then they left. Then the police turned up, someone else in the hotel called them, but the men who beat him had left by then. Then the police put what was written on the wall in their report. Then they took Jonker to hospital."

"You're right Swart, it's a terrible thing."

"No sir, the terrible thing was what they wrote on the wall – with the blood."

"Nothing bad about the railways I hope?"

"No sir, nothing like that. What they wrote was queer."

"What was queer about it?"

"No sir, that was the word 'queer'. That was what they wrote. Twice."

Sakkie Theron declined at once into feverish malady. He pulled the cigar from his face just in time to stop it being rammed to the back of his throat as he lowered his forehead dramatically to the desktop. Once slumped thus he hissed "Christ," through clenched teeth. Then he pushed himself back in his chair and directed a groan at the ceiling "Ooaaaaraa!" He jumped up and walked over to the wall, leaned his body into it face first and went "Aaarggh!" Then he stared out the window which looked onto the bleak station interior and shouted, "Why now?! Why couldn't he have chosen a better time to be a bloody pervert?! No! the fool has to be disgusting just in time for the prince's arrival. I don't bloody believe it!" He turned and faced a recoiling Harry Swart, "You know what this means don't you Swart?"

Nervous Swart confessed he did not really know exactly. "It means that the Jew will have to drive the bloody train, that's what it means!"

144

Leaving

Although he had lived with her, Mary had never been Eban's responsibility until now. He thought he would manage to ignore her like before somehow. But without the privilege of space in the home life was unbearable. After working on the farm each day, Eban would walk home taking a route away from the cottage rather than towards it. He'd think, pray or dance in the veld, hoping Mary would be asleep when he got back, but her sleep patterns were unpredictable and she sometimes stayed awake all night jabbering, harassing, irritating, goading, and drinking.

Eban had to leave. He wasn't taking care of his wife the way Thomas had wanted him to. His friend had thought he would be a good influence on her, make her right, but it was the opposite. It wasn't all her fault, he should never have married her. He should have told her the truth – that he didn't love her, that he was just keeping a promise to Thomas. He had been wrong. Cruel. He would tell her the truth. He must tell her the truth and then leave. The scene was not as ugly as Eban had anticipated. Mary, drunk, just laughed grotesquely and said that he was a bloody stupid bugger if he thought she didn't know why he married her. She spat in his face and showed him her arse and sucked the bottle she was holding dry then hurled it at his head. It smashed against the wall. Nothing too unusual. "Go! Get out of my house you bastard shitty bum from hell!" she wailed. Then she froze and stared and shed tears of genuine grief. Eban approached his wife and held her tenderly for the first time. She let him a moment. It felt wonderful to her. Then she scratched his face. Then he left.

Costumes

In Oudtshoorn fancy-dress was a serious business. It was most popularly inspired by Greek mythology and chatter about town made it clear that many Oudtshoorners were keen to repeat the theme at the royal event. However, the Royal Committee felt that a clear theme should be decided on to avoid togas mingling with tutus and making the whole thing "look like a bloody mess," as Thys de Beer put it just before his wife launched into her campaign for consensus on a single theme. "Thanks my darling," said Sara as she stood to make her high-pitched point. "Yes, we all know what everyone looks like in our Greek clothes," she said. "I think it would be much more exacting if we really thought of the most unusual creative costumes. We don't want the prince to think we are a bunch of stupid farmers what knows nothing about culture and art, do we?" Agatha sighed and muttered but one devastating look from the mayor – who had reminded her of the shameful information he cradled just half an hour earlier – and all she did was make a series of disapproving expressions by way of opposition.

"Yes so I thought, what would be the most fun thing? I hear the prince has a wonderful sense of humour and I thought what is the most fun and lovely thing? And I thought it would be animals. We could all dress as different animals." By the end of the meeting it was agreed that the theme was animals and that there would be a crate of champagne for the most creative costume at the ball.

Depite her determination to hate the idea, Agatha thought of her already worked out ostrich gown and struggled to suppress a smile.

Solutions

$\mathcal{S}$akkie Theron went to see his superior, Barry 'Boet' Visagie, and Boet Visagie sent a telegram to Nico Pretorious, his counterpart in George: ROYAL TRAIN DRIVER IN HOSPITAL STOP JEW ONLY OTHER DRIVER STOP WHAT TO DO STOP

Nico Pretorious in George tapped back: DON'T TELL VAN SCHALKWYK STOP JEW MUST DRIVE STOP BUT KEEP HEAD DOWN STOP SAY ROYAL PROTOCOL STOP SHIT STOP

"Well Isaac, I suppose you've heard about Jonker?"

Sakkie Theron winced and clutched at his heartburn as he spoke.

"Yes sir," said the Jew, struggling to disguise his delight "It's a bad business sir, you know, a very –"

"Yes, yes, I know Isaac," a mien of irritation pinching at his vocal chords.

"You are the only other man qualified to drive the royal train, but I suppose you realise that already."

"Thank you sir. Yes I did think – "

"Yes, well it's important that you know a few things. About the responsibility itself. Protocol. How it must all go. Stop fidgeting and sit man."

Ben sat and faced Sakkie Theron across a desk of chaos and tried not to move at all. Theron glowered back and flicked at a typed sheet of paper as he spoke.

"This is a list we've received from the royal household, telling us how to do things."

The page he held was in fact a letter from Mrs Swannepoel of Zebra, who had left her hat on the 11:45 train to Oudtshoorn two weeks earlier and wanted to know whether the railways had found it, and if not, then would all rail staff please look out for the thief, possibly wearing a large hat of purple velvet with a pink feather across the front brim. It was hers.

"They make it clear here," started Theron sternly, "that number one: no train driver ever speaks to anyone from the royal party Two: that those privileged enough to drive the prince never hang any part of their body out of the engine, especially when the party is boarding or leaving the train. That's no heads or elbows Isaac. Three: no talking to anyone along the way. Four: the driver must keep his identity top secret from everyone, even after the royal visit." Theron stopped and looked intently at the page wondering whether he should fabricate any more rules that might impress the driver with the importance of his becoming a ghost when the great day came. But nothing else came into his mind, not even Eva Groenewald, who generally occupied the space between his ears whenever the day paused a moment. Nothing. So he continued: "There are more, but those are the main ones that concern you. Now these rules are direct from the palace and so it is vitally important that we abide by them." He tapped the page importantly as he spoke. "Is it clear to you Isaac? You must not even tell your wife that you are the driver!"

"Yes sir, very clear sir."

The plan to keep the driver's identity veiled was futile. No matter how well he would keep his immaculate uniform and fluffy scalp out of sight on the day of the royal journey, the word was out within minutes of the news breaking that Isaac would drive. Everybody knew. Anybody knew. Even nobodies knew, and on his way home that evening Sakkie Theron felt his diaphragm twist when a demented drunkard lurched past him dribbling a song he had made up himself that very afternoon: "The Keeeng! Ees kuming! Eet's true! And the Jew! – ees going to drive heem!"

The twist in Sakkie Theron's body held at its most uncomfortable and he moved his top lip half an inch up his face without opening his mouth, and for the second time that day his imagination blurred without constructing the form of Eva Groenewald.

They must stick to the plan anyway. They must believe in the secrecy of the ghost driver. They must, if they were to avoid the fire and brimstone which would surely hail down upon them from Theolonius van Schalkwyk at railways headquarters in Cape Town the moment he found out. They must! It was their only hope of perhaps cooling the lava before it gushed along the track and into Port Elizabeth station and engulfed them all.

Thoughts

The royal train was due the next day. Eban was living in the mountains outside De Rust, meditating on the harrowing months past. His thoughts were chaotic. Too much had happened for there to be any clarity. How was the shopkeeper's wife? Was Thomas watching over him, distressed by his failure to save Mary? Mary would be drunk for sure. What about Angel? That hair. Those eyes. Ruth would be loving Hannes. Would Hannes speak now? What would he say if he spoke? Eban wanted to speak normally, then he could talk to Angel more easily. He also wondered where he came from, and why was he so black? Sister Helen – was she dead? Was he a bad man? He'd killed Van der Want and left Mary. Would the prince like his dance? What to eat?

Protocol

*N*ext morning Ben Isaac was up at five. Much humming filled the air as Hannah helped him into the rigid blue overalls, still set aside in case of just such a miracle. The funny hair was controlled with the help of half a jar of Vaseline, and the podgy cheeks were carefully scraped so not one nick botched them. His small round spectacles with the broken arm had been carefully mended with fine silver wire by Ben himself the night before. His hands and nails, ingrained with blackness from years of engine driving, were so scrubbed by Hannah that they looked pink and tender.

Ben left for work earlier than usual so he could stroll along slowly, savouring anticipation and avoiding sweat. Hannah waved him off then went back inside to prepare herself at leisure for the royal send-off at ten. When Ben arrived at the station the good ladies of the Women's Institute were draping miles of bunting all over the red brick Victorian building and what Ben later described as "thousands" of flower baskets prettied the place up too. The platform was beginning to look like an ornate interior passageway. Ben thought it was a wonderful thing.

But his chipper good mornings were greeted like something that made his colleagues itch, and he was only allowed to participate marginally in their excited preparations. It was hardly a new sensation for Ben, and he moved stiffly about, with a benign expression on his face, in a halcyon world of his own.

He had been told to report to Sakkie Theron at seven thirty, which he did. Theron, whose heartburn had, if anything, intensified during the night, was so struck by the starched and slicked Ben Isaac that he managed some compliment before easing himself painfully out of his chair.

"Thank you sir. Starch you know sir. Vaseline," said Isaac pointing to clothes and hair.

"What? Oh, yes. Sit down Isaac – if you can. Do you remember what I told you yesterday?"

"Of course sir: no elbows or heads or anything out of the engine. No chatter along the tracks. No looking at the royal party."

"Yes. And you don't disembark until the party has left Oudtshoorn station." Theron moved around to the coat-rack and dislodged his jacket.

"Yes sir."

"Nobody knows for sure who will be driving the train?"

Theron moved closer to Ben, holding his jacket by the shoulders.

"No sir."

"Good!"

Theron hooked the jacket over the driver's oily head and ushered him out to the train.

The prince and his party arrived fifty minutes late. They numbered twenty-three. Companions, aides, ladies of uncertain title, all magnificent, they all might have passed for kings and queens themselves. They appeared in a flourish of the type of regalia ridiculous enough to disappoint no one and a fringe of local dignitaries who greeted the guests as they emerged from a string of carriages looked frumpy by comparison.

The prince himself was short and highly unattractive. Very big nose, flaxen hair too long, lips too thin. He was also fat and displayed a gregariousness, maladroit rather than charming, which only highlighted his clumsiness. His non-regal bearing was further highlighted by one of his closest companions being a man of such abundant beauty he almost glowed. (A small girl in the crowd which lined the platform even pointed at His Highness and asked, too loudly, whether he was the handsome prince's jester.)

But the crowd, which had submerged itself in an orgy of romance around the hideous oaf for half a year already refused to exhale so much as a breath of disappointment, and they cheered and waved just as they had longed to. The prince fiddled with the feathers in the mayor's wife's hat, he touched the mayor's moustache, he even patted one large South African lady's behind, and he guffawed at all his own puckishness. The bewildered hosts were determined to appear accustomed to such tomfoolery and laughed their heads off at the most annoying man they had ever encountered. They even took to mimicking his approach.

They slapped their thighs when he did and opened their mouths wide as they could when they laughed. They bent themselves forward, and tinkered with his medals. The lady who had had her bottom tapped even drew the prince's sword at his bequest, almost beheading the mayor in the process. Such levity. Who could have imagined?

Ben Isaac had already been at the helm thirty minutes by the time the prince and his entourage were settled. Stock-still he sat, staring straight ahead, turning only his eyeballs towards the platform in the hope that the prince might cross his line of vision and perhaps even congratulate him on his turnout. He never did, and at the guard's signal, Ben moved the train off, as smoothly as if it had been running on soap.

In Oudtshoorn

That day in Oudtshoorn tempers soared along with the mercury. Tears and tantrums rippled through the town full of people dressed as dogs, lions, geese, chickens, goats, leopards, cats, snakes, fish, cows, sheep, tigers, gemsbok, springbok, duikers – and more.

The monkey suit Thys de Beer's wife had organised for him was too small. He had swelled a couple of inches since he was measured and had refused any fittings in the interim. Mrs Broil was called in to execute emergency alterations, which made the waistline looser but proved less successful around the gusset and the mayor remained uncomfortable. "This is just brilliant. I'm the mayor and I'm going to be spending the whole bloody day pulling my monkey tail out my bum," went Thys.

"Don't worry my darling," Sara reassured him, "Everybody knows that the monkey is the cleverest animal. I wouldn't be surprised if the prince isn't also dressed as a monkey!" For some reason this absurd platitude calmed the mayor and he sipped at his gin and tonic and periodically readjusted his tail without even noticing. It was a motion that would become more natural to him as the day progressed.

On the Rocks

Eban looked around. The mountains were orange. The grass looked like faded sage. The sky was bigger and bluer than anything. Eban could see the morning heat rising as intensely as he felt it. His mouth was dry but it didn't feel bad.

The royal train was due in five hours. Eban rose with the sun and walked about a mile to a large flat rock which jutted out from a cliff beside the track, about fifty feet up. He sat down and dangled his legs over the edge. He ate a breakfast of peaches he'd plucked from an orchard nearby. He hung his head back and squinted at the sky. He flicked through some images in his mind until he reached the one of the little prince, The Infant of Prague, and dreamed a while. After that he saw himself dancing. The dance he had seen in the river. The grace of it astonished him. He imagined the train's approach. From that height he believed he would be able to look down into the carriages as they passed. The people inside would look back at him. They would point and gasp and call the prince to come look at the man moving on the rock. He saw it all in slow motion, even though he knew that the train moved faster than a galloping horse, he knew they would see him, just like he had seen the dance – slow.

Silent Waving

*B*y ten o'clock the silent wave had already been rehearsed several times. "That was better," hollered Karel Prinsloo, "But I think the ladies could smile more prettily than that." The ladies were, for the most part, plain as rats' arses. The men were no better looking but nobody was asking them to be pretty. A few of the children could have passed for cute, but their new attire made them look like little white boxes rather than the small, agile creatures that they were.

"Alright now! There go the three warning toots!"

The crowd stood still.

"I told you, you have to imagine you hear them when I say that, and lean forward. There go the three warning toots!" The crowd shuffled into position their bodies at forty-five degrees to the track, their faces pulled into stiff, grotesque smiles and the ladies trying to look prettier.

"And here it comes! The engine has reached the edge of the platform!" Everyone's right arm shot straight up into the air, hands shaking furiously.

"And now the train is right along the platform!" Bodies moved round, like shop dummies on jerkily revolving pedestals, silent, grinning, waving, and turning more and more to the left. "And they're passing through! And past, and past, and away!" Arms dropped, faces drooped, old people were helped back into the shade. "That was better. Er, Mrs van Deventer, perhaps you could stand a little further back. That's right, just behind your daughter. A bit more. Like that, yes." Mrs van Deventer was an eyesore: bloated, rubicund, squint and warty.

To Dance

*E*ban sensed the train would be a while and relaxed in the shade of a bush. At two minute intervals he peered into the distance to check for its approach then relaxed again. Eventually there came a soft panting in the distance. He rolled onto his chest and watched the thin black iron worm slide closer through the giant landscape, towards him.

He brought his knees up under himself, and pushed effortlessly up onto his feet. He moved onto the precipice and bore the burning rock casually on the soles of his feet. His chest was bare. He pushed it up and out and let the sun bake it a moment. He frowned at the train getting closer and stood, pasted in the scenery, alert and hush.

With the engine about five-hundred yards away his dance was sparked. Eban moved slowly, the train moved fast. Eban stared down at the carriages. The perspective was so acute the engine seemed to be pulling nothing but a chain of black roofs. He kept moving regardless, certain that even though he could not see the prince, the prince would see him. Seconds later, the guard's van had turned its back on him. Eban kept moving. The choofing died, the steam evaporated, Eban stopped. His heart beat fast. He stared after the prince's train until the mountains swallowed it up. His mouth was dry but it didn't feel bad.

Fleeting

The boys with their ears to the track suddenly leapt to their feet and jumped and yelped. The De Rusters, bedraggled, sunburnt, thirsty, ribbons slack, hats askew, flew about the platform and tried to position themselves as rehearsed. Children, almost scruffy now, were slapped and shoved into position in front of marginally more presentable parents. Mrs van Deventer forgot to conceal herself and several men who had not been assigned to line the platform edge shoved their way to the front of the crowd.

At five minutes to twelve Ben Isaac's engine hurtled towards De Rust at full steam. No warning toot was let off and within fifteen seconds the royal entourage had clattered past the gaping villagers in a blur. One sex, one person, one lump of messy splendour flew past at a speed that seemed to the De Rusters like lightning.

The prince happened to be glancing in their direction at the time and glimpsed the eerie array of simple folk, wrapped in a wave of white muslin, grinning like statues. They appeared as one bizarre creature with a hundred heads and millipede limbs and a spine of hands swaying down its back. The peculiar sight, which had caught the prince's eye by chance startled the boisterous monarch into a rare state of contemplation. Unsure whether or not to believe his eyes and with nobody else seeming to have noticed, he held the image secret.

Postscript

The royal ball was the last great party in Oudtshoorn. Within six months of that glittering day Sara de Beer stood in line holding a wooden bowl and a tin spoon. Her dress of overpriced French silk, although still quite new, looked shabby, the two dozen pearl buttons having been removed and sold. The dress was pinned together and hung loosely about her – she had lost thirty pounds since offering the prince her hand and wobbling slightly as she curtseyed lower than was she could comfortably manage. The soup she waited for was a watery blend of pumpkin and potato cooked up by a group of kind Christian soldiers.

The second feather crash took less than a fortnight to set hard. The outbreak of World War One, and saturated feather markets left most of Oudtshoorn's rich, poor.

In the weeks that followed the bank's withdrawal of credit, the sound of solitary gunshots ringing through the wide Oudtshoorn avenues was not uncommon. The self murderers who didn't shoot, hung, or slashed, or poisoned themselves instead.

After one final plea to Patrick Bloomfield, Thys de Beer was among those who could not bear the shame. Bloomfield's final advice to the mayor had been to seek some kind of business alliance with Agatha Teeling-Smith: "I think she's going to invest in ladies hair products," said Bloomfield the second and final time the wits-end mayor visited his office: "That's what I heard anyway. I think there's a lot of money involved, she might need someone like you with all your contacts and all." De Beer was silent. Just hung his head.

"Maybe. I don't know. It's just a thought," Bloomfield trailed off, still looking away, through the window, onto a quiet, dusty, Thursday morning Main Street. When he turned back around, Oudtshoorn's big man had disappeared without another word. One bullet did the job twenty minutes later. Thys de Beer left no note.

Agatha Teeling-Smith did not have to queue for soup. She had had no children to educate, and had seen Europe long ago. She had filled her house with things of beauty and enjoyed driving herself about in a motor car, but otherwise there was nothing particularly decadent about her lifestyle. But she could not remain. There were too many people to help, how could she choose between them? So she packed up her house and her servant and left for Scotland. It was time to go home.

Jacana Media publishes a wide range of exciting titles: biography, history, fiction, business. Take a look at all our titles on www.jacana.co.za

A few of Jacana's titles are:

A Life of One's Own – Hilda Bernstein's story of one family disrupted by ideology and the force of history

A Fisherman in the Saddle – Julian Roup's meditation on the soothing delights of riding horses and fishing

The Serpent Under – a dry and gritty mystery by Rob Marsh

Lekgotla: The Art of Leadership through Dialogue – a must-have guide for South African managers by Willem HJ de Liefde

Johannesburg Portraits – From Lionel Phillips to Sibongile Khumalo – Mike Alfred's history of the city as seen through the lives of businessmen, artists, politicians and scientists

African Soul Talk – a debate between Rabbi Warren Goldstein and Dumani Mandela on citizenship, the African Renaissance, and values and morals in today's world

Power and Terror – Noam Chomsky's latest work on America's role in the world and the implications of the war on terror